U0110082

東鱗西爪

Patches of Light Clouds

王之◎著

作者簡歷：

　　王之，畢業於陸軍官校、國防外語學校英文班、淡江大學；在美攻取兩個碩士及匹茲堡大學圖書館學博士。早先，大陸變色，死裡逃生，曾服務於部隊，參與金門古寧頭、八二三戰役；後轉國防機構，任研究編譯。及至美國，曾服務於多所大學圖書資訊館，一九八九至九八年，為關島大學圖資院長，現為關大圖資正教授。作者學術論著甚多，在臺期間，有大陸政經等譯作五冊。後有圖書資訊等專論，散見於多種期刊及論文集；間亦撰寫散雜文，披露於中、英報刊；其部份學術論著及散雜文，經彙編成書三冊。

　　王博士早年服務軍旅，屢得勛獎章。服務關島，曾主持關大圖書資訊館擴建、自動化、引進新資訊設施、網際網路等。一九九〇年啟動及主持關島總督圖資大會，獲選為關島代表，率團參與一九九一年白宮圖資大會；並為美國國家圖書資訊委員會遴選為代表，審編白宮大會討論議題。

作者著作書目：

Electronic Publishing and Its Impact on Print Publishing: A Study of Expenditure and Usage in Three Selected Libraries in Atlanta, Georgia (A doctoral thesis). Pittsburgh, PA: University of Pittsburgh's School of Library and Information Science, 1988.

Guam Governor's Conference on Library and Information Services (A report). Agana, Guam: Government of Guam, 1990.

Government of Guam, 1981-1995: An Information Source. Mangilao, Guam: University of Guam's Micronesian Area Research Center, 1997.

Thirty-Years' Practice in Libraries: Recollections and Ruminations. Philadelphia, PA: Xlibris, 2005.

Guam and Micronesian Libraries: Historical Events, Information Sources, and Others. Philadelphia, PA: Xlibris, 2005.

《東鱗西爪》*Patches of Light Clouds.* 台北秀威科技公司，二〇〇五年。

書像降落傘，打開來，才能發生作用；
圖書館像所羅門王的寶藏，走進去，
才不會空手而歸。

好讀書不好讀書

—— 蔡元培

目　錄

散文 Essays

東鱗西爪

微言贅語 Notes and Miscellanies

閑讀抄摘 Reading and Reviews

趙　序

　　關島大學圖資館前院長王之教授，學術著作豐富；偶亦撰寫中英散雜文，抒敘人生經驗，談論世局時政，巂語連篇，鞭辟入裡。今選取重要部份，編印一冊，歉稱《東鱗西爪》。實際上鱗爪之間，含蘊離亂情懷，憂國氣志，夾纏時代血淚。曾國藩為歐陽生文集作序說：「文章與世變相因，俾後人得以考覽。」《東鱗西爪》，發自憂患，中西並容，經時代鍛練，烙下沉重腳印。

　　王教授出身農村，在抗戰戡亂的砲火中成長，弱冠請纓，陸軍官校畢業，曾參加金門古寧頭戰役，是八二三砲戰的守土將士。服務軍旅，屢得勳獎；後入普通大學，畢業成績，名列前矛。繼赴美深造，於獲得兩個碩士、擔任大學圖書館要職多年以後，毅然辭職，重返師門，近花甲，攻取博士學位。通俗而言，這是「九轉丹成；」其實，艱苦奮鬥中成長的人，對世道人生，體驗深刻，識見深遠。北宋名臣范仲淹，幼孤家寒，斷虀畫粥，寺廟埋頭讀書，終而領悟「先天下之憂而憂，後天下之樂而樂，」以天下為己任的社會價值觀。抗戰期間，軍民穿草鞋，愛國情深，突顯了孟子「生於憂患，死於安樂」的意義。

　　書中有趙校長，似曾相識，卻緣慳一面。該篇文字活潑，報導真實，激勵國家賢良，鼓舞海外忠義，文章載道，文公含笑。（趙）文披露不久，關島便有臺北經文辦事處，也是巧合。其餘〈牧童、老兵、花甲博士〉、〈在美被搶和訴訟〉、〈德國統一及其與東鄰的關係〉諸篇，看到作者生於憂患、經歷文武、為人處事、奮鬥不懈的經歷；也窺見士人君子，讀聖賢書，犧牲奉獻，關懷故國的心路歷程。某文人雅士，以劉邦先入咸陽為謎面，影射作者名字。王之不是劉邦，未王天下，也是歷盡烽火，闖拼海內外；而王亦旺也，作者亂世逃生，意志旺盛，學業文章，興旺非凡，令人敬佩，令人神往，特為之序。

美國喬治亞州亞特蘭大

華聲報發行人　趙增義謹誌

Foreword

Following my husband's career in U.S. Navy, I came to Guam in 1991, and later met Dr. Chih Wang at the University of Guam. My first impression of Dr. Wang was that of a gentle and cultivated scholar, a fitting choice for his position as the Dean of the University's Learning Resources. Dr. Wang received regimented training and disciplined work habits from the Republic of China's Army Academy and during his military career. That experience, combined with the free-spirited environment in the U.S. universities where he earned his degrees, molded a model of "east meets west".

I was honored when Dr. Wang asked me to write a foreword for his book Patches of Light Clouds 東鱗西爪. In my living room, there is a perfect place for me to sit and relate to the pages from Dr. Wang's rich life. Facing me is a Chinese scroll painting of an ink dragon by Huang Shan-shou,. In this traditional brush and ink painting, hints of sharp claws, well-defined scales, and the body of a powerful dragon circulate among patches of light and airy clouds.

The history of dragons is as ancient as the Chinese people. Ubiquitous and ever-changing, dragons richly reflect the fertile imagination of the Chinese culture. The collections in all three parts of Dr. Wang's work articulate the person he is. Some, like a dragonfly skimming the surface of the water, send out endless, pondering ripples. Others are like the art of leaving un-brushed and un-inked spaces to form clouds in Chinese painting. The "non-being" includes the unlimited possibilities of "being". What's important is the essence contained therein. The vacant has substance.

The memories we choose to share are the only true spiritual legacy we may give. They are like seeds in Nature: each a wonder, a summation of all that is.

Christine Ku Scott-Smith, Director
Learning Resources, University of Guam

前　言

　　本書《東鱗西爪》，收集保存筆者部份中、英雜文、散記等，分編三部份：散文、微言贅語、閑讀抄摘。散文有筆者浮生略影，見聞點滴。雜論有摘譯一篇，略述東西德統一經過，以及一些時事管見。最後部份為閱讀介紹和抄摘。各篇空間，外加一些插植。

　　筆者生於鄉野，資質魯鈍，適逢亂世，少時了了。未及冠而從戎，曾於金門古寧頭、八二三等彈雨中，浴血支撐過臺澎的生存；生命精華時光，獻給了中華民國。歸去來兮時，流落異鄉，為衣食溫飽，庸庸碌碌；孺慕藝林書海，但欠深緣。一生浮萍，漂遊東西，一些涉獵、收集、日誌、書札，或為風雨浸沒，或因搬遷散帙。本書所收，為筆者後後半生散雜文和書札等，其中多篇，已散見於中、英報刊。翰海涓滴，無足輕重，敝帚自珍，聊以為自修、自勉、和自慰而已。

　　收集當中，有一部份為英文，為編印方便，全書採用西式橫排。書後備有索引，便於查考。

　　感謝上蒼憐憫，世亂時艱，得以溫飽偷生。感謝眾多兄弟姐妹和親友，在人生艱困路程中，給予支助。特別感謝吾妻、吾女、吾兒，無怨無尤，跟隨左右，時刻扶持。

PREFACE

The monograph collects my selected essays, notes, and miscellaneous writings. Many of these discourses appeared earlier in various publications; some of them were my mind exercising pieces. Like the patches of light clouds scattered over the erratic sky, these collected works were the minute inklings in my oscillating and evanescent life. The collection might serve as a scribbling pad, where the petite pulses of my mind and body were jotted down in different times at separate spots.

Many thanks are due to my friends and colleagues, who helped me one way or another in my life and career, particularly to those who assisted me in putting together this monograph. Special gratitude is given to my wife, Kwei-yung; my daughter, Marianne; and my son, Henry for their understanding and support of all my endeavours in my life.

散　文

ESSAYS

But **WORDS** are things, and a small drop of ink,
Falling like dew, upon a thought, produces
That which, makes thousands, perhaps millions, think.
— **Lord Byron**

小名

　　生逢亂世，因為避秦逃亂，冒頂了一個名字，久而久之，假名取代了真名，原來的名字，反而廢而不用了。反正身為無名小卒，阿狗阿貓，都無所謂了。

　　西洋人的姓氏，有鐵匠木匠，以工作職業為姓。猶太人很多金匠銀匠，所以很富有。中國人取名字，習慣上依從算命相士，批排八字，不是用金用土，就是福祿壽喜，希望五子登科，光宗耀祖。筆者雖為帝王姓，冒頂而來的名字，卻非多年萬歲；之則是一個虛字，缺金缺土，無寶無玉，不沾榮華富貴，也不招男招弟，毫無意義；而且「之」字形狀彎曲，頭頂千斤石頭，注定筆者一生東奔西跑、漂泊負重的艱困道路。

　　之字雖無意義，卻屬中性，不像糞土或羚羊，沒有什麼不可登大雅之堂，也不算怪名。其實之字可作助詞，與王姓連用，正表現華夏王道精神。朋友好玩，曾戲作「劉邦先入咸陽」為謎面，影射筆者姓名，可見筆者小名，亦非全無意義。

　　這個小名字，也有好處。遇到以姓氏筆劃排名時，筆者就常名列前矛，獨佔鰲頭。朋友有三兄弟，以一、二、三為名，可惜他們姓萬，姓和名加起來，筆劃就多了。丁姓朋友，若以一、二、三為名，筆者便要屈居下峰了。

大概名字簡單，外交部倒有一位真王之。這位先生不但外交事業很有成就，西洋文學亦有造詣，曾在某大學授西洋古典文學。當時筆者亦在同校選修英文，真假王之雖未謀面，同學卻常引為話柄，說筆者沒有避諱，不尊師重道。多年前，寫雜文應景，收到回應，討論主題外，并詢及美國國會圖書館內情，丈二金剛，不知所云。原來小名英譯，與國會圖書館王公大名，僅多了一點後尾，掠人之美，汗顏不已。

昔在鳳山望雲山麓泥地裡打滾時，某次一位袍澤生病住院，全班簽名捐款慰助。當時生活十分緊張，時間分秒必爭，筆者倉促簽名，遞交鄰兵。班長平時緊拉馬臉，不苟言笑，這天看了筆者的簽名捐款，面部略略鬆弛一下，慢吞吞地宣佈，五元捐五元，全班聽了，雖不敢張牙露齒大笑，大家都不禁莞爾。從此以後，同學經常伸手索取五元。

近有台灣朋友來訪，相聚聊天，不忘國內習慣，連連叫之公、之公，叫得一旁女眷，粉臉通紅。

以上閑聊說笑，說了便罷。使用了多年的名字，不管是真是假，再要更換，則不是好玩了，尤其要和官府打交道，更是麻煩的事。報載南港有女潘金蓮，請求改名，戶政機關認為沒有充足理由，駁回不准更改，新聞媒體傳了開來，潘女士才得易金為玉。最近發現，國內兵籍檔案，把筆者改為王文，一點交叉錯誤，拜託了朋友，上了千言書，費了九牛二虎之力，聽說還煩及了部長，積年累月，始得改正過來。

牧童、老兵、花甲博士

同樣的年齡，前輩已統率軍旅之師，我卻剛入伍，在南部望雲山麓泥土地裏學打滾。差不多的年齡，許多人已是教授或校長，我卻於每天工作之餘，追擠公車、火車，和小朋友輩一起背書包，上夜間部。今日花甲將至，本是歸去來兮，準備領取授田而耕的時候，我卻不自量力，強取一個博士頭銜。是許多身體殘障朋友的鼓勵，他們或以輪椅代步，或有目不能視，有口不能言，卻克服重重困難，力爭上游。也是阿Q自編的道理：太多的事都遲了，但若遲晚便罷，歲月並不會因此停頓下來、不往前行。

我是牛頭班元老學生

不知誰是沒有根的一代，只知我是屬於沒有名堂的苦難一代。中國歷代梁山英雄眾多，我們的舊社會也有太多的好漢和豪傑，我們這一代出生來世，華夏錦繡河山，因為群豪爭霸，已被破壞無遺，民生教育，淪於破碎邊緣。自有記憶開始，我每天都與牛為伍，割草打柴，毫無小學教育可言。若有牛頭班，我是元老學生了。補習，慨嘆升學壓力，是當年難以想像的。

　　接著，日本鬼子的侵略戰火，燒遍南北；烽火連天，機聲隆隆，一天三番兩次空襲警報，驚惶不定，怎樣上課念書？沒有親眼看到南京大屠殺，沒有目睹重慶防空洞內、千萬人窒息而死，但我永遠不會忘記，鬼子走了之後，我的家，我的學校，被燒被劫；一片燒剩的瓦礫，餘煙繚繞。沒有家舍，沒有學校，一點餘留的夢想，全被燒盡了。

　　日本人走了，東方又昇起了一個紅太陽，另外一群「英雄好漢」，把華夏僅餘的人、財、物，砸個稀爛粉碎。又是一陣激烈的槍砲，又是一次無情的殘殺，在恐怖絕望之中，我離開了鄉土，離開了學校；沒有一分一文，沒有半紙文憑，從此之後，天涯海隅，無處為家。

　　在閩浙高山叢林的路途中，我曾看到倒地不起，痛苦呻吟的人馬；我自己的骨肉兄長，就在那裏悲慘離去。在閩江口外海，我曾搭乘於一葉漁舟，漂浮於洶濤狂浪之中，度過無數晝夜；一位手足兄弟，竟爾落海而去，為巨浪吞噬。在廈門外海，我嘗受過海水煮食的味道。在鼓浪嶼附近的小渡船上，我曾為隔岸的砲火擊中，幾乎葬身魚腹。

深夜流的淚，吞回肚裏

　　不知是幸運抑或不幸，一江山和登步島戰役，我都避開了。但是古寧頭和八二三砲戰，卻適逢其會，也是參與的一分子。古寧頭之役，人潮來，人潮擋，兵學家或有很好的分析，我只知我沒有倒在那灘頭，屍首沒有為茅草所裹。八二三之役，我也沒有追隨吉星文將軍，在太武山公墓佔一席地。但在地下泥洞裏，在壕溝中，我和其他的千萬軍民，曾頂過了數萬發、如雨而下的炮轟。某晚，十二點停止砲擊的時限愈逼愈近，料羅灣碼頭，沒有燈火，鴉雀無聲，四周死寂，世界好像停止了呼吸，灘頭只留下我和三數難兄難弟，隔岸若果放一串鞭炮，我們大概都在那灘頭餵魚了。

　　古寧頭戰役後，我闖到了臺灣，曾於基隆十八號碼頭打過尖；也換過身份，滲雜於眾多女眷之中，以士林戲院為棲身之所。對門好人家，憐憫我無依無歸，曾打開大門，讓我借用他們祖壇前面的一塊泥土地，作為我夜晚歇腳的地方。

　　為了生存，能夠走的路，我都走過，可以找到的零雜工，幾乎都做過。有時夜半流出一滴眼淚，我都用唇舌接起，吞回肚子裏。記得為了去中山南路補習，常深夜一人，步行越過中山橋而回大直。那時電視沒有問世，收音機稀奇可貴。想盡了方法，弄了一台聲音沙啞的三手貨之後，我遂開始收聽每天清晨三十分鐘的英語教學。但是同房室友，群起反對，罵我國語說不好，反而學洋涇濱，要做洋奴。

先輩以五百支步槍、打倒軍閥

數載成長，我正式進了兵營，和許多不很年輕的朋友，開始學習吸氣、收肚和挺胸的立正工夫。這群朋友，大部分都是一時英傑，各有不同的來歷。有人躲藏於大汽油桶裡，從澎湖脫逃而來；有人險被裝進麻布袋，拋棄於馬公外海；有人穿越西南崇山峻嶺，歷盡盜匪洗劫，百死一生，脫險而來。相形之下，我的一些膚淺經歷，能算什麼？

按照傳統，兵營長幼有序，新兵向老兵行禮。後來的高中留美班、大專預訓班，不管傳統和秩序，他們理直氣壯，質問老兵，誰有初中文憑，誰有高中證書。從此而後，新兵老兵，路途相遇，只有鼓起雙眼，相瞪而過。我們一群流離孤兒，能爭什麼？

憶初進營時，曾聞有科學、哲學和兵學混成教育一說。不知誰一覺酒醒，要辦新制，於是舊制成了敝屣。反正先輩以五百支步槍，一雙草鞋，都能打倒軍閥，戰勝日本。我們有精神教育，已經足夠，科學和哲學不屬於我們這一代。因此，我們被遺忘於一邊。

一張有去無回的機票，來到新大陸

政治本是把戲，不使花招，坐不到舞台的中央。戲台上一片鑼鼓，我這個僅拿一面小旗的兵卒，也被精簡了。翻閱報紙廣告，發現所有公私機構，只收三十以下的大專畢業生。某公幼女，十七八歲，肄業於淡水河邊某私立中學，得到銀行的金飯碗，是為例外。為什麼限年三十，若不是有意排斥我們這苦難的一代，又是根據什麼人事理論？我們的社會，從來沒有過問就業歧視和機會均等的問題，其中是否也另有道理？

沒有三分薄田可耕，沒有辦法謀取一分工作，現實逼人，只有冒險來美一途。以全部退伍金，加上一些朋友的幫助，於是買了一張有去無回的單程機票。到了新大陸之後，便跑去唐人街附近的周某傭工介紹所，賣身做零工。好在遠隔重洋，沒有熟識的朋友，頭不低，臉不紅，進了門，便找個位子坐定，和來自五湖四海的眾多朋友，一起等候差遣。

放牛牧童，來到大千世界

一個窮鄉僻野的放牛牧童，來到了大千世界，太多的新鮮事物；嘗盡人生百味，只是從無甜食而已。紐約市縱橫交錯的地下鐵路，閉起眼睛，我可分辨出南北去向；踏破鐵鞋，我跑遍了曼哈頓、長島、牛爾克、紐約市內外。我曾雜處於各路英雄之間，賃陋室於時報廣場中心，身陷花花世界，出污泥而未染。中外餐館，洗碗、打雜和跑堂，十八般武藝，我都嘗試過。前人筆下大菜刀的威風，「我不愛爹娘，我只愛關老爺」的老板娘風彩，也看了不少。以前在兵營裡，曾以三個月薪資，闊充食客，學習洋食禮儀。現在身臨其會，以不同的位置，我才分清楚咖啡和奶油碟，咖啡匙和湯匙，五花八門的起士，和各色強軟飲料；屈身於陰暗的餐館地下室，被叫三聲老王，聽起來別有一番味道；躑躅於百老匯和華爾街，眼前只見高樓連天，人來人往，猶如螻蟻而已。

　　一串漫長的驚夢，醒來已是夕陽西斜。昔日南部兵營驕子，今天已是公卿大夫，老兵仍在掙扎，在異域的土地上，重新學習打滾，沒有什麼可以炫耀，也沒有什麼可以遺憾。人生際遇不同，到盡頭大概亦不過如是。荷馬《伊里亞德》中的阿契里、莫維爾《白鯨》中的船長阿海布、海明威《老人與海》中的老人，歷盡創傷，故事末了，有何不同的結果？人生如是，每個人只是盡其在我而已。金蘋果在那裡？白鯨的奧祕，還有老人為什麼祇拖回一串大鯊魚的龍骨，不必打破沙鍋，追問到底吧！

松露是人間美味，卻深藏在森林間；

至美的情境，往往也要慧心才能相遇。

吹笛人說：「要用心去吹，把生命吹出來。」

我們活著，也要用力去活，讓生命的笛音悠揚動聽。

—— 羅任玲

＿＿＿＿＿＿＿＿＿＿＿＿＿＿＿＿＿＿

堅實好看的樹木，都被砍走，

剩下來有裂痕、沒人要的木頭，

長久活下來，就成了神木。

神木本是沒有用的散木，做船會沉，

做棺木會腐朽，做梁柱會生蠹蟲，

因為它無用，才長得高壽。

神木「無」用，

無掉世俗之用，才得成全神聖的用，

無掉人為之用，才得回歸自然的用，

無掉世俗流行之用，才得保全自己理想的用。

無用之用，是為大用。

—— 王邦雄「神木無用」

AN ORDEAL OF A LONG JOURNEY

It has been a nightmare for Hillman since the ordeal occurred over many years ago. His heart beats fast and his pressure runs high every time when he awakens from the dream that, covering with a white sheet, his body was frozen on a stretcher being carried to an ambulance.

In a chilly morning after being at home in Atlanta for a few days, Hillman reluctantly got up at four o'clock and kissed off his wife and his teen son although they hardly opened their eyes. This was the third time he drove from Atlanta to Pittsburgh since he went to school there. He knew the road well; about sixteen hours, he would be in Pittsburgh to resume those copious but boring classes, reading, and writing.

It was still dark and the night was whispering and dreaming. Having a cup of black coffee beside him, Hillman sat behind the wheel, driving about 70 miles per hour as soon as he got on I-85 north. Before long, his mind was sinking and tears blurred his view. Why should he have to separate himself with his sweet wife and young son to take this long and lonely journey?

Passing through towns after towns, turning from highway 85 to 77 and 79, and dragging for a prolonged day, Hillman pulled his car into a rest area and took a break at the border of West Virginia. Without his radio on, he soon fell into a dream in his drive seat and was back again with his wife and son in Atlanta.

The lights were flickering when he opened his eyes. After yawning and stretching out, he sulkily started his engine and moved his car back to 79, heading towards West Pennsylvania. Six or seven more hours, he would be in Pittsburgh. But now clouds were piling up over the sky and the wind was gushing in the wood. Snowflakes began drifting in the air and carpeting the highway soon after he was in the mountain.

Before long, the snow poured down like a gush of cotton balls falling out of the immense upside-down containers from the heaven. Hillman was soon besieged in a world of snow. Everything was wrapped in white; trees posted like giant patrolmen and tall Gothic buildings. Rebounded from the shine of the snow on the ground, the sky turned wickedly pale; and the night transformed ominously chalky. The highway was buried in an ocean of white; Hillman could hardly trace and follow the driving lanes of the road.

Except snowing, the world was dead; no any other single car or any other single living being was seen around. Eagles disappeared; they must be napping in their comfortable nests, coiling of their sour wings. Squirrels were hiding; they must be secluding in their secret cells, peeping at the asininities in the planet.

Hillman was vacillating between leaving and staying on the highway. Without snow tires and adequate equipment, driving downhill on the white-covered slippery exit would be suicidal. And fastened in his mind was that he would have two classes and a paper due in the next morning.

He was also awake that he would soon be paralysed by the freezing snow and buried in the mountain should he stop there. He had to keep on driving, moving his car forward inch by inch. He glanced at the gas meter, that told him he had only about one-half tank of gas remaining in the car, and it became less and less each time when he peeked at the meter.

He was overwhelmed and had no idea when he

could get out of the snow-piling mountain. His mind was wondering, searching for a way of survival. A flow of cold abruptly ran down his spine when he recalled the news report of two international students, who were frozen in their automobile in a New York mountain last winter. Covering with white sheets, their bodies were vividly appearing before him as they had been seen in a TV report.

Hillman strived every second to concentrate his attention on the steering wheel and figure out the lost drive lane in the amassment of snow. After toiling for hours, he spotted a gas station appearing on the right horizon on about the same altitude of the highway. Like a lighthouse to a wrecked ship in the middle of the rough ocean during the dark night, it brought the hope back to Hillman, who sturdily managed his automobile to the station.

Having his tank filled and his mind rekindled, Hillman was on the perplexed highway again, thinking that he still could catch up his classes at Pittsburgh. After another hours of vigilantly ploughing in the snow mud, he was out of the mountain. The day was dawning; the snowdrift in the sky began dissipated; and the snow bank on the road, thawing. A few other phantoms of automobiles were seen hopping on the horizon.

Hillman took a deep breath but still held on his wheel firmly and conscientiously. Instead of plunging in the snowbound highway, he was now entrapped in a river of muddy snow broth; therein the steering wheel was not wholly under his control. The temperature was below zero; but his underwear, soggy. A few inches of distraction from the road, he would tumble to the deep bottom of the vacuous valley.

Inescapably, a stumble took place. To evade hitting head on a stack of yellow mud on an ascending ramp, Hillman slowly and slightly stepped on the brake. His car was then out of control and swiftly veered to the left. Like a helicopter, it swerved into the air, bounced over the road rail, turned around, and landed in the ditch on the side of the road. He thought he was gone. Astounded but awakening, he instinctively raised his right hand and felt around his head to see if he was bleeding.

After being rescued, Hillman was back on the road continuing on his perilous expedition. Having stubbornly and stupidly drudged in the overwhelming white for extended hours, he finally arrived at Pittsburgh, where he

sighted the Cathedral standing gracefully and majestically over the sky of the university campus.

After being dragged and drifted in the dreary world for a long while, Hillman is now more perplexed and confused than before. He could not figure out how he got out and why he had to take that long, muddy, and perilous journey.

ETCHED IN STONE

Echoes in the Night

It was one night on Quemoy in September 1959 when the enemy scheduled to resume its artillery bombardment starting at 12:00 midnight after a recess from its fanatic assault of previous weeks.

Lights were shut off and the moon disappeared. Dogs were hushed and people wormed into underground. The night fell in a dark room, except a few far-away stars secluding behind the blackened clouds. The tiny island was dead, only insects there muffled now and then.

Beetle was posted in a foxhole in a valley. He peeked his watch almost every second. The needle trembled towards the point from where a time bomb would trigger off. His pulse ran fast and he could hear his own heart beating.

Suddenly, a glare of light pierced over the sky. Swiftly followed was a crash sound of thunders, bommm, shaking the ground, deafening his ears, and immersing his mind. The pandemonium pounded the surrounding hills

and reverberated in the hollow back and forth eternally.

Awoke by his phone buzz, Beetle focused his attention, looked towards the source of the horrible explosion, and tried to conceive what had happened. Was a bomber shot down, a gas depot detonated, or had the enemy commenced storming at the isle?

Dumbfounded, Beetle breathed the smell of the blood that once painted the Normandy beach, and sensed the distant vibration of the a-bomb's crushes at Hiroshima. Echoing in his ears were the perpetuating wails of burning down of the Ching's Palace when the barbarians invaded Beijing in 1860, and of the Ching's battleships sinking in the Yellow Sea when they were shattered during the Sino-Japanese War in 1894.

A Stranger in the Night

"Beetle." Chill ran down his spine when he was still dazing in his foxhole and heard someone calling him. The voice was shivering, eerie, but familiar. He turned around. Sergeant Wood's phantom was in the trench haunting towards him.

It was under that dark shadow in the same ditch one day last week that Sergeant was dragged out. He was blown up by a bomb exploded nearby, when Beetle was one or two feet away from him, talking about the *War and Peace.*

Like having a gallon of crimson paint pulled over him, the Sergeant's body was bathed with blood. His face was decomposed and two limbs were chopped off. Still he was groaning, "Beetle, Beetle," when he was being carried away.

As an enlist man with Sergeant for months, Beetle saw him hurdling over one hundred-pound bombs into cannon barrels like playing basketballs. In the first night when he was assigned to a patrol post in the shoreline, Sergeant took him there and told him where he had wrestled with "water ghosts," the frogmen dispatched from the satanic forces.

Under the eclipsed light of the camouflaged stars, Sergeant's silhouette was hovering closer to him. A needle in his heart, Beetle held back his tears, trembling and pondering: "Sergeant, are you back from the hospital or ashes?"

Etched in Stone

It has been about one half of a century since Sergeant Wood returned to the trench after he was shattered. Since then, his apparition has possessed Beetle perpetually. During these long years, the Sergeant's scarlet blood-bathed body that had returned to the ditch emerged and vanished before his eyes time after time on a bright day when he was toiling with inanities or in a chilling morning when he was falling in a nightmare.

Every time when Sergeant loomed around, he kindled Beetle's mind, recollecting those days when they were at the marine base or in the battlefield. It was that year that Sergeant coached Beetle and transformed him from an innocent schoolboy into a grown man, a valour soldier, who was chosen to deplore in the fatal front line.

"It was another quiet night," Sergeant was chattering here and there. He was inspecting his men at the seashore. Suddenly, he heard the water was splashing, alerted that they were landing, and crouched down to the ground behind the shadow of a bush. Like a gush of wind, three water ghosts whirled over the reef, quickly advancing towards the beach about fifty yards away.

"H O L D!" Sergeant thundered at them. Two of them froze there instantly. One manoeuvred to run away. "Pon, pon, pon," he crushed, and the other two surrendered.

It was one day about three months after he enlisted, Beetle recalled clearly. Sergeant exposed to him a tiny seashell when they were chatting while doing chores at the base. It was shining, smooth, and graceful with a hue of human touch. "It was found at the Cape Hope." Sergeant commented. "It must have been ground, crushed, and smashed by the relentless waves for hundreds of years. It has been an invaluable and adorable jewel in my family for over fifty years."

Beetle does not know much about Confucius or Socrates, but Sergeant's effigy, valiant stories, and especially plain words were etched in stone, which have become the beacon guiding his life.

五十肩和泡澡塘

　　兩年以前，出外糊口，牽手沒有隨身照料，夜間睡眠，為冷氣吹襲，左肩膀受了風寒，開始酸痛不舒服。拖了幾天，病情每況愈下。左邊脖子、左肩骨，甚至左手全部，都有僵化現象，行動痛楚，很不方便。沒法度，只得去求醫生，接受X光透視，打針又服藥。朋友見了面，說是五十肩，要我每天早晚，甩手三十六次；並大口保證，三十六天有效。晨三十六，晚三十六，手甩了，三十六天也過了，五十肩還是五十肩，一肩不少。

　　三十六天漫長難受的日子裏，時常想起多年以前曲姓朋友的經驗。曲兄生長於北平，到了臺灣，不習慣於亞熱帶的氣溫，炎夏時節，經常蓆地取涼，以電扇吹眠。為時不

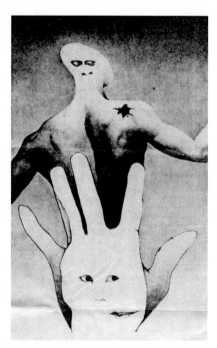

久，終於中風，全身癱瘓。朋友的痛苦印象，歷歷在目，受了恐佈的壓迫，我只好請假回家，找牽手想辦法。回到了家，白天讀讀寫寫，窮忙一通；傍晚整理庭院，搬土除草，修剪花木。每天弄個汗泥夾背，再回屋內，打開熱水，沖一個痛快的涼。然後坐定，任由牽手捶打肆虐；酸痛刺辣，真是滋味無窮。說也奇怪，不到三十六天，五十肩竟消聲匿跡，不治而癒。牽手為我看相算命，批斷我勞碌命，五行之中，注定做苦力；骨頭下賤，不打不捶，會出毛病。

幾個月以前，我這個好動的石頭，滾來了關島。這裏位於南太平洋，有高高的椰子樹，白淨的海灘，熱帶風光，優美媚人，自然不在話下。但地近赤道，氣溫和濕度偏高；而室內裝有冷氣，因此，室內室外，好似炎夏隆冬，形成強烈對比。初從內陸來到的人，很難適應。來了不到一月，五十肩反撲，襲擊另外一個肩膀。如同兩年以前，一樣酸痛，一樣難受；又是醫生，又是針藥，但都不見效果。經朋友推荐，改看針灸醫生。經一番診斷把脈，醫生搬出了中醫經典，說第六神經受了壓迫，並樂觀表示，經針灸治療，很快可以痊癒。

醫生朋友，推拿針刺並用，極為認真用心。又是三十六天，效果卻不理想，我也失去了耐心。朋友又建議，不妨試試馬殺雞。但是一翻當地報紙，發現關島的這項行業，也是天下烏鴉，有純與不純之分。報紙有顯著廣告，馬殺雞行業，高張艷幟，鼓吹美女如雲，為客親熱服務。我初來新到，人地生疏，恐怕闖錯了門戶，到時吃不消，無法應付事小；弄壞了我的五十肩，使我癱瘓不起，則要遺憾終生了。尤甚者，若被愛死，見了閻羅王，還帶了一臉灰；因此，謝了朋友的好意，沒有去接受按摩治療。

又有朋友提供意見，說有個大旅館為諾魯共和國人經營，不是日本商人經營，內有健身房，設有各種運動器具，流動熱水池和乾烘房，勸我一試。朋友盛意，無法推卻，於是每個週末，便跟著朋友，一起去做運動和泡洋澡塘了。每去，我先在健身房逗留一、二十分鐘，挑選一些器具，活動頸項，肩背和手臂。然後去澡塘和熱烘房。

沒有去過西安，沒有泡過華清池，不知貴妃湯如何；離國時間久，也不知三溫暖的名堂，無法把這個洋澡塘和故國名池相比較。記得以前當兵時，曾跑過臺灣南北，泡過各地的公共浴室，包括北投的公共溫泉。這個大旅館的澡塘，雖屬公共，卻不是以前泡過的那些浴室可以相比。這個澡塘有浴池和噴水間。浴池的熱水，滾滾流動，任客調整溫度和水量，進入的熱水，帶著強大壓力，由浴池四周衝刺而來。噴水間水龍頭的來水，壓力強猛，打開之後，水勢或像一連串彈珠，傾注而下；或像針刺，兇猛壓迫而來。

跳進浴池，對著不斷衝入的來水；跑到噴水龍頭下，或站、或坐，讓作怪罷工、活動不靈的筋骨，任由熱水猛沖猛刺。十或二十分鐘以後，平臥於澡塘旁邊的躺椅。放鬆肌肉，看著滿身汗珠，一滴一滴外流；這時候，外面的繁雜事務，也隨著流失的汗珠，遺忘於天邊。水池泡，水槍沖前後，時或躲進熱烘房，或打坐，或躺臥，讓乾燥熱氣，烘烤五、六分鐘，則又是一番風味。一房騰騰熱氣，看不到，摸不著，但卻感覺真實，團團圍繞全身。待不多久，先覺肌膚灼熱，然後血脈膨脹，唇舌枯乾。坐立不安，只好撤出，退回外間的澡塘世界。連續的運動操練，連續的沖泡烘烤，經過了幾個周末，五十肩一肩肩飛去，我也轉移陣地，到游泳池游泳去了。

躺在澡塘旁邊的涼椅上，看在眼前，想起往事，發覺現實和想像，兩者之間遙遠的距離。以前年輕力壯，血氣方剛，聽聞東瀛男女共浴，腦海之中，曾激盪過漩渦，想入非非。現在親身經歷，與黃白男女，雜處共浴，大家三點兩點，僅遮去少許罪惡的源頭，倒是心湖平靜，是怪不怪了。這大概就是惑與不惑有了區別。

　　其實，澡塘、泳池和海灘，地點互異而已，前法於後，都是兩點三點，有甚麼不同。再者，男男女女，近看不如遠瞄，大家含蓄遮去一點，保持適當距離，隱隱約約，或者更美，更有韻味。而且，到健身房運動的眾男眾女，醉翁之意，大部分還是在於酒。進了健身房，推、舉、拿，大家勞筋勞骨，個個汗流夾背。進了澡塘，熱水泡、熱氣烘，筋骨酥軟，醉翁即使別有意圖，丹田元氣，也不容他或她，興風作浪，為非作歹了。而我，田雞一隻，有目無珠，不戴眼鏡，咫尺之隔，不分男容女貌，眼前是男是女，穿多穿少，幾無區別。同時，澡塘裏溫度大、熱氣高，即使架起眼鏡，貪圖一探究竟，眼前卻是霧是霧，花非花了。

　　以前少不更事。聞前輩朋友，泡澡塘，作賤揚州鄉親，每次逍遙，半天一天，心中不以為然，暗罵他們懶散、墮廢。如今，自己由少輩而前輩，流落於太平洋的一個伶仃孤島，受五十肩困擾，也墮落於澡塘，每去一泡，總是三、四個鐘頭。經過幾次熱水猛沖，醍醐灌頂，頓然覺悟：泡澡塘、推拿和捏腳，是柴米油鹽以外，一項重要的生活藝術。

　　我們販夫走卒，擠身前輩之後，難免庸俗纏身，勞於刑役，往往心力交瘁，常有不支之感。這時跑去澡塘，沖泡一、二小時，外加一番純馬殺雞，忘去塵囂，讓筋骨肌肉，心肺內臟，鬆弛擴張，重新調整一番，再酣睡一夜，然後去開會酬酢，處理案牘，解決人事糾結，或為中副寫篇短稿，賺一點臺匯臺援，貼補買菜，保證輕鬆愉快，事半功倍。讀者若身列前輩之林，生活緊張，工作繁忙，不管有無五十肩，華陀再世，也會奉勸你去一試活動熱水澡塘。

感謝上蒼，藉五十肩的折磨，讓我覺醒，悟今是而昨非，明白禮失求諸野，泡澡塘、捏腳和按摩的中華古老文明，雖沒有在故國故土，受列尊敬重視，卻在五湖四海，發揚光大，不僅對症下藥，治好我的五十肩，而且是醫療緊張繁忙，現代文明病的良方。

開車意外事件後記

某日，太太請客，交下菜單，限期採購；為國民外交，帽子大，奉命之後，駕車遠征，去三十英哩外的東方雜貨店。一路無話，平安到達。

辦好豆芽菜、春捲皮等南北、葷素雜貨以後，時間已經不早，晚間還有其他要事，急急發車，加速油門，取高速路回駛。上得路來，平時車輛風馳電掣的八線大道，現時卻是車水馬龍，擠得寸步難移。原來，時間已是下午四點過後，交通擁塞的尖峰時刻了。擠進了車堆，進不得，退更難，急得混身是汗。

費盡了九牛二虎的力量，忍耐著比螞蟻爬行還慢的速度，最後回家的出口岔道，終於遙遙在望。一時欣喜，暗忖不負老婆的使命，大概又可以得到一個輕快的香吻了，動作稍快，也耽誤不了晚間的約會。突然前面長龍一條，停下不動了，怎麼辦？瞬間，眼睛瞄過後視鏡，發現左線一個缺口。快加油、扳方向盤，車子一下換過了線。卡擦，格格格，碰撞聲，緊急刹車聲，遲了，遲了，不知那裡橫過來一輛車子，擦過了我的左邊，斜停在前面，是一部新卡特萊克。對方車主下了車，我也下了車，馬路零件橫陳，不用看，都是我們車上分身掉下來的。老美藍眼圓瞪，鼓鼓的，差點掉出來，嘴上的毛，翹過了頭頂，怒氣沖天，朝我走來。而我，驚天動地之餘，也還鎮定，不自覺地向他伸出了手，是歉意，還是為了緩和空氣？

　　警察一時沒有來，老美也沒有飽我西洋老拳。沉默片刻，我頗有意和平解決，告訴他兩造難逃過失，不如各修各車罷了。老美名駒受損，大概傷痛及心，不肯接受，並且掏出了紙筆，記下我的姓名、地址、車號等等，好像過失完全在我，一切非賠償不可。和平既無希望，只有靜候警察處理，等待打官司了。

　　回到了住處，車子鼻青眼腫，不用問，便知發生了甚麼。消息傳出，朋友跑來安慰，也為我提心吊膽。數星期前，張三撞了車，刮了對方一條線，賠了千元，又李四怎樣，王五如何。一連串的報導和經驗，進洋法院，面對洋法官，說洋話，按情度理，這場官司輸定了。對方又是全新名牌轎車，價位很高，事情非同小可，如何是好？

　　審判的日子到了。生平沒有到過法院，沒有動身，心已跳出了胸口，跳歸跳，提著心、背著膽，還是準時趕去了。到了法院，候審室裡門庭若市，坐的站的，堆滿了人，大概有了伴，一路忐忑的心，平靜了許多。不久，終於來到了審判庭。法官高高在上，額頂白髮，約六十開外，白胖的臉，不像包青天，卻似彌勒佛。第一件案子只有單方到庭,當事人坦承過失,買有意外保險,願意承擔賠償,三言兩語,約一分鐘結案。

接著,我和對方當事人,來到了判案前,由洋人領先,申述事件經過,報告車輛損失。然後由我比手劃腳,結結巴巴,陳述一番。然後由當時處理現場的警察作證。他們說些甚麼,我沒有聽得十分清楚。法官好像在聽,卻滿不在乎,沒有拍案子,輕輕地說了一聲,各自走路。洋車主聆聽之後,一聲未吭,扭轉頭便走了。我不明就裡,打破沙鍋,追問到底。大概法官日理萬幾,類似芝麻綠豆,清官難斷,看了我一眼,判定各自負責。

現在事已過去,只是車子的傷痕,留給我一次難忘的經驗。回憶檢討,那天要是這樣那樣,這場意外,或許就不會發生了。車輛碰擦以後,我和洋人的態度,也是兩人文化細胞的自然流露。我要息事寧人,洋人卻要鑽牛角尖,實事求是。其實,這種公有公理,婆有婆理,說不清,理還亂的官司,包公再世,也難判斷。難怪法官見怪不怪,面對這些千千萬萬的日常事件,大概都是一聲「阿門」,解開大家庸人自擾的結,赦免眾罪。

在美被搶和訴訟

陳大姐出國觀光，經過舊金山，錢袋被搶了；王姥姥來美探親，在紐約國際機場如廁時，有人從門外奪走了她的皮包。在這文明的黃金國裏，盜匪如毛，信不信由你。筆者曾混跡於紐約市碼頭，虎口討生，常以老美國自居，向來不把盜匪搶劫的事，當作與我有關。又是一則地方新聞，報導搶案。這一次被搶的，不是陳大姐、王姥姥，而是筆者本人了。

話說不久以前，筆者和內人在外糊口，旅途歇息於一小鎮的汽車旅館，時間不過是晚上九點多鐘，外面有人敲門，筆者適在衛生間，內人沒有經驗，開啟了門。說時遲，那時快，筆者於衛生間出來，內人已在槍尖下俯伏於地。筆者出來，也只好隨之躺下。匪徒於是翻遍箱籠，拿走了全部現金、信用卡、駕車執照、和汽車鑰匙。幾經週旋，與虎三番謀皮，匪徒竟然有動於衷，手下留情，丟下現鈔二百、卡照和鑰匙，這也是我們中國人所說的盜亦有道了。

被搶之後，丟錢受驚，心中自是懊惱；沒有用上中國功夫，制伏洋匪徒，尤感耿耿於懷，一時極不愉快。旋與旅館理論，要求賠償。要生意人出錢，的確難如駱駝穿針孔。搶匪尚有商量餘地，旅館經理卻一口咬定，說筆者開門揖盜，一切應該自己負責。旅館非但分文不施，房錢仍全部照算。

旅館關起了門，沒有談判餘地，要追索賠償，唯有尋求法律途徑了。經過接洽，一位律師應允予以研究。拖了一個月，回覆是，本案勝訴機會不多，不願出面告訴。再洽第二個和第三個律師，反應相同。多位同事和朋友，私下相告，他們眼看這個旅館起高樓，前後不過六個月。言外之意，旅館業主多半是地頭蛇，沒有人願意一捋虎鬚。

失望之中，某日發現一本小冊子，題為小型申訴法庭自訴程序。小冊不過十數頁，說明小額損失受害人，可向該庭提出自訴，一審終結，不須聘請律師。經過三番細讀，依照程序，起草一信，寄給旅館，說明原因，正式要求賠償損失。旅館相應不理。

一星期之後，遂往指定法院，填妥表格，向小型申訴法庭，提出自訴。旅館接到法院通知，警覺不能置諸不理了，於是聘請律師，出面抗辯，不肯庭外和解。接著，法院裁定日期，通知訴訟雙方，到庭辯論。筆者不習法律，對於六法，一法不通；受老祖宗凡事三緘其口的教訓，口齒又甚笨拙。面對旅館財團和「醜陋的」美國律師，用洋文，打洋官司，內心的確恐慌。但事已至此，總不能退堂罷休，貽笑於老外。事不由己，於是蒐集了許多有關書刊、法令和判案，不分晨昏，勤加鑽研。

開庭日，筆者站立於控告席，先申述搶案經過，提出有關佐證，指明旅館沒有適當安全措施，要求賠償被搶的損失。被告律師否定控告，拒絕賠償，理由是：

（一）旅館設有安全保險箱，房間有保險鎖。

（二）控方的損失，係因自己疏忽，開門揖盜，以及沒有利用旅館安全設備所引起。

（三）旅館業主並非旅客財物的保險人，通常情形，不執行警戒責任，情況必要，是為例外。

（四）本州沒有旅客被搶、旅館賠償的「類同案例」可循。

被告律師退席，法官、法警、書記官和旁聽人的眼光都轉移了方向。在這緊要時刻，唯有勇字當頭，挺起身，把數星期來惡補得到的資料，胡謅出下面一大堆理由：

（一）法院多有判例，認為社會情況改變，防範罪犯，已成今日工商業的日常事務。法學家亦主張，處於今日社會，讓受害大眾，承受所有犯罪負擔，是不合情理的事。比較合理可行者，為讓社會犯罪的第三者，負起責任，防範罪犯於未然。

（二）查警局過去六個月資料，被控旅館範圍之內，曾發生犯罪案件多起。根據今日社會的現實，以及被告旅館本身的經驗，旅館業主應該知道，犯罪案件，隨時都可發生。事實已明顯地構成了必要情況，應該執行警戒，業主卻疏忽責任，沒有執行應行的措施。蓋搶案發生當時，被控旅館既無安全警戒人員，亦無電動安全設備。

（三）根據委託保護理論，旅館業主為旅客財物的委託保護人；承受委託，應採取措施，防護旅客財物，若有不周，引起損失，應負賠償責任。

（四）旅館既未公告安全保險箱，亦無招貼，警告附近的治安情況，對於防護旅客安全，已經失責，因此之故，應依委託保護的普通法理，對於旅客的損失，負責賠償。

（五）法院有百餘年判例，裁決旅館賠償旅客損失。早有一八五八年德州法院引用委託保護的法理，近有威州判例。威州判例，與本案大致相同。

（六）本州近有判例，捨棄「類同判例」之說。準此，被告律師所提本州沒有「類同判例」可循之抗辯，已無立足理由。

（七）孫子有云，止戰於敵國，為國防上策。今日美國不惜巨大費用，維持海外基地，理由在此。待敵人戰火燒近門前，大勢晚矣。早期警戒，適時行動，為國防必須的負擔。國防如此，旅館防護旅客安全，亦復如此。坊間討論旅館安全的著作頗多，大致重點，均強調防患於未然。本案事實證明，旅館疏於防範在先，而導致匪徒得行其道於後。

幾經唇舌，被告律師節外生枝，循詞強辯，謂控方所指各節，或適用於一般旅館，非汽車旅館。並提出抗議，謂本案不屬小型申訴法庭管轄，應移交民事法庭審理。

辯論到此，塵埃大致落定，筆者於是輕鬆相答，指出所有著作和判例，通稱旅館為備有設施，提供旅客住宿者，概不分此旅館和彼旅館。至於法庭轄權，為程序問題，應於進入訴訟之前提出；現辯論將告結束，已無討論餘地。

辯論終結，被告律師趨前和法官握手言歡，多位法警和旁聽朋友，則圍著筆者，抬起眼目，細眺一位說英文不忘中腔中調的中國佬。

一星期後，接到法院判決書，旅館也由律師轉

來支票一張，被槍損失，外加庭審費用，全部賠償。
損失得了補償，欣喜不在話下。身為炎黃子孫，沒有
適時使出功夫，固屬遺憾；單槍匹馬，舌戰洋律師，
取勝於旅館財團，贏得洋官司，也聊為海外的中國兒
女，舒一口氣。

THERE'S A REASON

For ev'ry pain we must bear,
for ev'ry burden, ev'ry care,
there's a reason.

For ev'ry grief that bows the head,
for ev'ry teardrop that is shed,
there is a reason.

For ev'ry hurt, for ev'ry plight,
for ev'ry longly, pain-racked night,
there is a reason.

But if we trust God, as we should,
it will work out for our good;
He knows the reason.

Tabor Cards

面談面面談，面面談面談

　　所謂面談，也就是口試，我們一些升斗小民，或求學、或謀職、或相親，有形無形，多少都會經歷幾次。求學和相親事，相去已遠，筆者記憶模糊，這裏且免談了。

　　窮為升斗小民，我們大部份都沒有在臺北擁有一尺土地，一坪房產；我們不是諸葛武侯，沒有人三顧茅廬；今日世代又變，除非賭氣餓肚皮，我們已沒有首陽山可以采薇而食。為了三升五斗，我們一定都會接受幾次面談或口試，出賣自己，折盡腰肢。

　　許多年前，讀過一篇散文，描寫一位面談人折腰的窘態。接待室風吹心動，一舉一止，都引起了面談人的聯想。坐在裏間辦公室太師椅上的是不是面談的主持人？是男是女？帶一副關公臉，還是像一個豬八戒？他問東，如何答西？一連串胡思亂想之後，面談人的眼睛終於落到了通往裏間那扇門的手把上，輕微地卡擦一聲，他的心沉下了一千丈，隨著掉進了無底的黑洞，所有應對腹案，也全都忘記了。

　　流落美國多年，筆者學了一點滾動石頭的道理，也嘗了不少面談的辛酸苦辣。早先數年，幾乎有面談約會，總難免失眠三晝夜；到了面談的現場，往往心

跳手軟，張口結舌，對答問題，不知所云。後來經歷
多了，應約面談，還能盡其在我，相信這裏不留爺，
自有留爺處；不再把成功和失敗，看得很嚴重。所以
面對難題，可以從容應付，心安理得。這也許是過了
老夫子所說的不惑之年，患得患失的心，少了一些的
關係。

　　記得某次去南加州、鄰近沙漠地的一個小城市應
試面談。出門以前，筆者已把有關的資料，翻查閱讀
了好幾遍。到達了目的地，又買了一份地方報紙，看
看當地的新聞，以作最後準備。那天的頭條地方新聞
是地震。現場報導，歷史記錄，筆者都快讀了一遍。

　　到了面談的會場，三男四女，已坐在一條長桌的
兩旁。筆者坐定，經過了寒喧和介紹，便言歸正傳，
問題出來了。筆者強裝鎮定，抬起眼睛，橫掃一遍，
然後頓了一下，學著老外，於回答問題之前，來一番
討好賣乖：「貴地風景好，環境十分刺激，沙漠近在
咫尺，風沙滾滾；今天又有地震，驚動天地……」幽
默未完，主持面談的眾男女，面面相覷，臉多改色。
不必問結果，剩下的面談過程，都是多餘的了。

　　幾個月後，筆者又重振旗鼓，遠征美國東北部。
有了前車之鑑，這一次不能再糊塗了。當面談官問
筆者為什麼千里迢迢，有意從南轉北時，筆者胸有成

竹：「新英格蘭是美國文化的發祥地，哈佛、麻省理工和耶魯等著名大學，都匯集在這裏，本人希望有幸，也能分享一點這裏高度的文化氣息……」這樣的如簧之舌，非出於筆者本性、也抹殺了早期印第安民族的文化，但不這樣窮白，又如何希望於三升之外，多加一粟呢？

數年以前，筆者又驛馬星動，四出另找新飯碗。這一次來到了紐約，面談的地點在一家餐館裏。強軟飲料，杯盤交錯。氣氛看似輕鬆。一杯未了，一位老兄有意無意，冒出了話題，問筆者貴庚。「年齡的祕密，恕不奉告。」沒有多加思索，來一個封關，其實這位教頭知道，循規蹈矩，他不應該問起國籍和年齡等個人身分問題。

一陣哈哈之後，另一位仁兄緊迫盯人，詢問筆者的思想趨向於保守抑或自由類型。「這個麼……」筆者慢吞吞地回答說：「自由的保守型。」對方張口大笑。沒有等候解釋，一位東方烘先生毫不饒人，問筆者在睡夢之中，使用英文還是中文。蒐盡了枯腸，筆者只得登七星山，求救于右老了，說當年有人問右老，夜間睡覺時，美鬚放在被裏面還是被外面。大家哈哈捧腹一番，一頓酒飯也就消遣過去了。

面談是成是敗，牽連的因素很多。如果面談官是個馬臉，性格保守，面談的人貧嘴烏白講，則注定失敗了。但一般而言，面談成功的要素，是要能夠隨機應變，風趣而不傷大雅，面對重要問題，能夠處之泰然，談笑自若。當然，輕鬆和風趣的背面，要有知識和經驗作後盾。

這一點，當今總統府資政蔣彥士博士極有修養。某次，蔣資政以教育部長身份訪美，在招待僑教界的一個餐會中，一位年輕朋友問當時的蔣部長，回國之後，是否將出任院長。蔣博士沒有否認：「是的，高雄可能會增加一個新的衛生院。」原來問題所指的是行政院，當時由蔣經國先生主持。所提的問題，肯定與否定的答覆都不十分適宜，頗為尷尬不好回答。讀者諸君，若有蔣資政應對問題的修養，大概也可以昂首闊步，乘電梯，登高樓了。

華美見聞

　　美國社會種族繁多，除了土著印第安人和歐洲移民的白人之外，有黑美、墨西哥美，和華美等等，紅黃黑白雜處，所以有人說美國是一個大熔爐，也有人說它是一個大拼盤。其實白美、黑美，和華美雖然居住於同一塊土地上，各個種族，有形無形地，都保有自己的社區，維持各自的生活習慣和傳統文化。所以近來有人又起了一個新名詞，形容美國社會是一方漂亮的鑲嵌品。

　　這方鑲嵌品，五顏六色，的確奇異漂亮。美中不足的是，各個種族相處，並不十分融和，尤其白種人，優越感重，輕視其他種族，因此種族之間，相互歧視，形成了這方鑲嵌品上的一塊大黑疤。以下片段，摘自好友黃炎的日記，所寫所記，雖是好友個人的經驗和思想，也代表了許多中國同胞在美國社會的辛酸苦辣。

不久以前的故事

　　客斯卑是黑人大牌電視諧星，家居好萊塢的庇福來山莊，左鄰右舍的房地產，價值連城。客斯卑心血來潮，偶爾亦親駕割草機，自己整理一番庭院。他每次割草，都穿著整齊，三件頭的西服，外加花色領帶。朋友心中納悶，問他賣什麼葫蘆。客斯卑有點生氣，回答說：「我在消遣，做運動的時侯，不希望有人打擾，要我為他們割草」。

* * * * *　　　　　* * * * *

何鴻稍有積蓄，在洛杉機拓展事業，開了一家中餐館，請來攝影師照相，準備作廣告使用。

「請稍微移動一下，這邊視角較好。」老美攝影師到後，何君禮貌地趨前打招呼，向他建議。

「去廚房炒菜，你那門子，懂甚麼照相！」老美眼珠長於頭頂，沒有側目斜視一下，大著嗓門，吼了回去。

何君是當時好萊塢大名鼎鼎的電影攝影師。

* * * * *　　　　　* * * * *

多年以前，顧維鈞博士往訪紐約市的朋友，敲錯了門。房內女主人透過了門上的安全眼，瞄了一下，隨口應說：「稍等。」稍頃，門打開了，女主人朝着顧博士的面，遞給他一大包髒衣服。顧博士傻了，但很快反應了過來，面帶微紅，告訴女主人說：「美國的洗衣店，可能都是中國人開的，但中國人不都是開洗衣店的。」

顧博士當時是中國派駐聯合國的首席創制代表，後來曾任國際法庭法官。

＊＊＊＊＊　　　　　　＊＊＊＊＊

某天，紐約市的警察、於五十二街攔下了王安的坐車。

「在那家餐館打工？」一眼瞄到是老中，警察大人二話不說，脫口先問開車的人。

「駕駛執照？」然後正經八八，檢查駕照。

「華爾道夫午餐回來，」王一面掏執照，一面漫不經心的回答。

「我在那邊上班。」王稍微抬了抬手，指著斜對面的大樓。

「你是王先生？」警察看了執照，又抬起了頭，看看那邊的（王安大樓）；腦子裡仍在猜疑：王安是老中？老中也有王安？而且在紐約市黃金地段，還有地標大樓？

滴點在心頭

在一間自助洗衣店裡，五、六個洗衣朋友，分坐在兩條長橙上，有黑、白男女，等洗等烘。一位白兄，烘衣機發生故障，沒有猶豫，沒有遲疑，不問左，不問右，直接的朝我走來，問我是不是店裡的工人。心中頗為不快，但我卻沒有顧大使的機敏。

＊＊＊＊＊　　　　　　＊＊＊＊＊

「貴姓？」

「姓夏。」

「那裡人？」

「康州人。」

「康州人？」

「美國人。」

「但是你姓夏。」

「我父、祖都姓夏，他們移來美國已有一百多年了。」

這是夏兄和一位白人推銷員在電話中的對話。

＊＊＊＊＊　　　　　　＊＊＊＊＊

從亞城前往華府的飛機上，認識了湯姆。湯兄熱誠，喜歡中國朋友。坐猶未定，沒有裝摸作樣，說什麼天氣，便急不欲待，說他愛好中國菜。一路一句多鐘，我們飽享了春捲、餛飩湯，和炒飯。

＊＊＊＊＊　　　　　　＊＊＊＊＊

從紐約飛往波斯敦，又碰到一位熱心的朋友，一路的話題，又是蘇絲黃餐館、中國城飯店，和幸運餅。

*****　　　　　　　*****

　一位白兄相問：「中國人刮不刮鬍子？」

「刮。」

「剃不剃毛？胸口的毛、腿部的毛。」

「不剃。」

「中國人的體毛，比我們白人的體毛少，為什麼？」

「雷根總統的毛髮多，還是猩猩的毛髮多？」

「我們比較接近獸類？」

「我們大家都是衣冠禽獸，中華民族或許古老一些，但你們顯現得性感多了。」

「開起玩笑了。」

「不然的話，你們許多朋友的毛髮大概長錯了地方。」

*****　　　　　　　*****

　小韋在美南小城大學圖書館工作，昨晚來電話聊天。他說，那天上午有兩個新生找他，查詢圖書資料，他們受到服務之後，沒有說什麼。這時適巧有人在一旁的複印機影印文件，兩個新生便轉向他，把原來的問題重複了一遍。小韋認識這位白兄，是隔鄰百貨公司的工友。

「後生小子好玩，不必太認真。」

「不是好玩，」小韋認真的說。「我有記錄作證，我們如有二人在資訊服務台，前來查訊資料的學生，絕大部份都不會找我。偶爾找我，他們也經常轉向第二個人，查證一番。那第二個人以及與我同時坐在訊問台的服務員，往往是我的助手、實習生，甚或不相干的阿毛阿狗。」

掛上了電話，心裡起伏不平，夜半輾轉床第，為小韋失眠。

* * * * *　　　　* * * * *

小韋又來了電話，訴說前往另外一個小城，接受面談，希望另謀生路，但是沒有成功的經過。他說，主持面談的人，指他說話帶有腔調。接著他提高了語氣地說：「季辛吉去面談，也沒有希望。」

「你錯了，」我提醒他。「季公是明星教授，又掛個名牌中國通，重要的是，他在新大陸，有歐洲白色的血緣。」

* * * * *　　　　* * * * *

其實，小韋已在他的行業服務多年，學位一堆，出自名校。學術界流行寫作發表，否則無法立足，小韋混跡其間，出版的文章，不是車載，也是斗量。相聚一起，朋友都勸他改行洗衣做廚。翻看華僑歷史，自從美國開發西部，直到如今，這是大多數中國同胞惟一可以糊口的行業。

＊＊＊＊＊　　　　　　＊＊＊＊＊

近幾天的地方報紙，連續出現「種族歧視」和「偏見、貧窮，阻礙進步」的大標題，黑人加克遜、布朗，和赫里斯卻都是大名頂頂的政、黨，和宗教領袖。中國同胞在那裡？埋頭在洗衣房、餐館，或實驗室？莫維爾小說白鯨中，船長阿海布和水手轟轟烈烈，日夜與白鯨搏鬥周旋。中國人浮影一現，無聲無息，始終都躲在底層的艙房中。今天，在美國的中國同胞是否仍如往昔，還是深埋在船艙底下？

THE DIARY OF A CHINESE-"AMERICAN"

Stories

Bill Cosby once was asked why he dressed in a three-piece suit while he was mowing his lawn.

"Man," Bill responded. "I don't want people to stop my work and ask me to cut their grass."

* * * * *　　　　　* * * * *

James Wong Howe called a photographer to take publicity shots of the exterior of his newly decorated restaurant.

"Could you please move to this corner so you will have a better composition?" Howe walked over and asked the photographer when he arrived and prepared to take shots.

"Go back to your kitchen. Do your cooking. What the hell do you know anything about photograph?" The photographer shouted.

Howe was a renowned Hollywood cinematographer.

* * * * *   * * * * *

An Wang was stopped by a policeman at a turn in the 52nd Street in New York City.

"At which restaurant do you work?" The policeman asked without a second of thinking when he noticed Wang as a Chinese. "Your license?"

"I had lunch at the Waldorf. My business is over there." Wang pointed at the huge landmark sign of the WANG building a couple of yards away while he handed over his driver's license.

"You are Mr. Wang?" The policeman asked when he looked at the license.

* * * * *   * * * * *

Willington Ku knocked a wrong door one Saturday morning in a Park Avenue Apartment in New York City. A woman looked through the peephole and responded: "Wait a second."

A few minutes later, the woman opened her door and handed to Ku a basket of bed sheets, panty hoses, bras, and other dirty clothes.

Ku, a veteran diplomat and the Head of the China's

delegation to the United Nations, was stunned, but he understood quickly and said: "I'm sorry, lady. All laundries in the country may be owned by Chinese, but not all Chinese here are laundrymen."

1980s

Today, when I sat on a laundry bench with several other folks waiting for clothes drying. A woman must have some problems with her drier. Without any hesitation, she walked directly to me and asked if I worked there. I told her I was sorry, but I did not have a second job in the laundry business.

$$* * * * * \qquad * * * * *$$

"What is your name?"

"Hsia."

"Where are you from?"

"Pittsburgh."

"No, I mean your nationality."

"American."

"But your name...?"

"That is my father's and grand father's name. They have been in the States for more than one hundred years."

This was a telephone conversation between Mr. Hsia and a saleswoman.

* * * * *   * * * * *

In an air trip from Atlanta to Washington, D. C., I made a good friend. We did not begin to know each other by talking about the blue sky. Instead, he was so happy to see a Chinese that before he actually touched his seat next to me, he had began to tell me how he loved Chinese food. Egg rolls, wanton soup, fried rice... we enjoyed Chinese dishes in the entire trip.

* * * * *   * * * * *

In another trip from New York City to Boston on a bus, Susie Hwang, Chinatown, fortune cookies... I was again enjoyed Chinese food with a mainstream American.

* * * * *   * * * * *

In a post office when I was reinforcing with a string a small package sent to California, a gentleman extended his hands to help me. After spotting the addressee, he pointed out to me:

"You ain't right, CAL not CA."

69

"Ain't this correct?" I wrote CAL on a piece of paper and showed it to him.

"You're VERY correct." He said.

"You're a VERY perfect fellow." I thanked him wholeheartedly.

* * * * *　　　　　* * * * *

"Learning a new language, particularly learning Chinese, is not easy." A Sinologist lectured in a third-year Chinese class at a well-known university in New England.

"We have learned the words 'east' and 'west.'" He wrote the two Chinese words on the blackboard.

"You know they are two opposite directions. This side is east, and the other side is...?" He pointed to his left and then to his right side.

"West," students responded.

"Good. The English Department is on our...?"

"East."

"And the library is...?"

"West."

"Very good. We are in the middle. We are 'not east not west.'"

Again, he wrote the four Chinese characters on the

board and asked students to repeat after him.

"We are 'not east not west.'"

After they chanted the phrase four or five times, the Sinologist continued on.

"However, when the two words come together, 'east west,' they are neither 'east' nor 'west;' they become a phrase meaning 'a thing.'"

"The chair is a thing; the blackboard is a thing; but human beings are not things."

"Now, please repeat after me."

The Sinologist lectured in Chinese, and asked the class to read loud the simple Chinese sentences he prepared in large writing:

"A book is a thing."

"A pencil is a thing."

"Human beings are not things."

"I am not a thing."

"You are not a thing."

"We are all not things."

✻ ✻ ✻ ✻　　　　✻ ✻ ✻ ✻ ✻

"Do you shave?" One of my good friends asked me this afternoon.

"Yes," I answered.

"Do you shave your chest, legs...?"

"No."

"Why you Chinese do not have so much hair as we do?"

"Who have more hair, Reagan or chimpanzees?"

"You're saying that we're animals."

"We're all animals. Perhaps Chinese are older people. But you look sexier, don't you?"

"You're kidding."

"If you don't believe me, I'd say you might grow hair in wrong areas."

＊ ＊ ＊ ＊ ＊   ＊ ＊ ＊ ＊ ＊

Wee called me from a rural town. He told me that this morning he was working with two young students at the reference desk in a library. After they received the information they requested, the two students turned to a white by a copier for the same question. The person they turned to was a sale clerk from a nearby department store.

"Don't be serious," I told Wee. "They're kids."

"Not really," Wee said.

"If I work along with a white," Wee added, "library

patrons will mostly go to the white for information. They may come to me occasionally, but quite often they will go to verify information I provided with a white, who may be a colleague librarian, a student assistant, or even an irrelevant person."

"Is that so?" I hanged up the phone.

✻ ✻ ✻ ✻ ✻   ✻ ✻ ✻ ✻ ✻

Wee called me again. He told me he went to an interview for a position at a rural college. He said he did not get the job.

"The director asked me what language I speak in dreaming, Chinese or English."

"What language would Henry Kissinger speak when he is dreaming, German or English?" Wee talked very loud.

"You're wrong," I told him. "Kissinger is a great scholar, and he also has kinship on this Promised Land."

✻ ✻ ✻ ✻ ✻   ✻ ✻ ✻ ✻ ✻

"What language do you use when you are counting the number in mind, Chinese or English?" Wee was asked in another job interview.

Wee has been in his profession for many years. He has had a handful of degrees, some of which are from top universities. In the world of publishing or perishing, he also has produced pounds and pounds of garbage to demonstrate that he is also one of the intellectuals.

Still, I always encourage him to go to laundries or Chinese kitchens, where have been the businesses a Chinese can survive in the United States since the transcontinental railroad was being constructed.

＊＊＊＊＊   ＊＊＊＊＊

Headlines in today's newspaper: "Racism's sting, prejudice, poverty remain barriers...." However, Jesse L. Jackson, Ronald H. Brown, Barbara Harris, Toni Morrison, etc. are all great names. Where are Chinese- "Americans?" Are they still in laundries, Chinese kitchens, labs, or in the bottom cabin of Captain Ahab's whale hunting ship?

1990s

The Great Wall, the Forbidden City, the crowd of people.... Joe seated himself next to me in a cafe and began to pour out the many stories of his recent visit to China.

"Do you know Mr. Chen?" Joe asked.

"Yes, I know many Mr. Chen's."

"He is a good man, not very tall, working very hard...."

"Where is he?"

"I met him in Shanghai."

"Do you know John?" I challenged him.

"Where is he from?"

"New York."

"Ha, ha, ha."

We enjoyed the whole Sunday morning.

$* * * * *$ $* * * * *$

"Here in the *Modern China* is an excellent article by Duck Doug on Deng Xiao Ping and the movement of modernization in China." Lao Mei was excited.

"Let me see it." Lao Chung asked.

Lao Chung took the journal and read the article quietly.

"It looks like the paper that I submitted to Duck one year ago for the course of Modern Chinese History."

"Did he re-write it?"

"Yes, a couple of punctuation marks and articles."

"You must have gotten an A for that class."

"I almost failed."

Duck is a well-known expert on the contemporary Chinese history at a prestigious university. Chung had been an assistant to Deng for many years before he became one of Duck's students after the Tienanmen Square Crisis.

＊＊＊＊＊　　　　　＊＊＊＊＊

Wee called me and said that he was drifted to Guam a couple of weeks ago. It seems that he is happy and excited on Guam. He described the exuberant hotels, the shining white sands, and the gorgeous ocean waves there. He said that with a pair of slippers, a short, and a towel on his shoulders, he could walk in and out of any high-rising hotel without being questioned as a stranger.

"Why?"

"Well, the hotel attendants will usually open doors for me, bow their heads humbly, and greet me 'konnichi wa' or 'konban wa.'"

＊＊＊＊＊　　　　　＊＊＊＊＊

* * * * *   * * * * *

P.S.: The diary is originally compiled by using the WANG computer and software.

亞城華人基督教會的亮光

亞城華人基督教會為亞特蘭大華人基督信徒聚會崇拜的許多個教會中的一個。七○年初，亞城華人不多，喬州理工的幾個學生，借用學校學生活動中心的一間小教室，開始主日查經崇拜。不久，人數漸增，查經班搬到學校鄰近的一個教堂，繼續查經崇拜，並有證道、見證、禱告、青少年主日學等。

三十年來，查經班的人數，不斷增長，早已成立了教會，建立了自己聚會的教堂。教會一搬再搬，信眾越來越多，教堂越建越大。近年以來，信眾超過千人，星期崇拜，教會從早到晚，分堂、分年齡、分語言聚會。東南西北，還有分區聚會。今年，蒙神允諾，北區開始分堂聚會，現正建堂之中。在神的帶領下，預期中還有其他分堂。

亞城華人基督教會的建立、興起和發展，為主耶穌作了美好的見證。基督教會肇始之初，神要在羅馬、以弗所建立教會，把基督的道，傳揚於外邦之地，彼得、保羅、巴拉巴便去了那裡。七○年代，神要在美南華人稀少的亞城，建立華人教會，便在那裡不斷撒播種子。

起初，神帶領了幾個年輕、同心、愛主的基督徒，來到了喬州理工。隨著，或因工作調動，或因信歸主，神又在亞城陸陸續續的召喚了更多的華人志工，共同參與亞城教會的事奉。這班兄弟姊妹，精力充沛，士氣旺盛；充滿恩賜、能力，更富愛心。多年以來，教會或有試煉，或有分心，他們始終憑著禱告、信心、和主耶穌的愛，成了亞城基督教會變動成長中的磐石。

亞城教會成立以後，先後主要有陳、邱二位神僕住堂牧會。陳牧師初到亞城，教會創建伊始，他和師母皆以傳道奉獻的愛心，服事教會。陳牧師誠摯、謙卑、木訥、寡言；但靈命深厚，熟諳真道，站上神壇，以一、二經句，深入淺出，反覆引諭，可侃侃長談；且常為兄弟姊妹洗腳，貶抑自己，引諭幽默，令信眾和慕道友捧腹不已，因而深為神所喜愛，為主在亞城教會奠立基礎。

邱牧師溫文儒雅，曾來過關島教會，大家相識。他和師母到了亞城之後，華人基督教會大大復興，信眾超過千人，不但教會本身蓬勃發展，增置分堂；且早已向外差傳，使主的恩典，分享亞、非、南美許多角隅。陳、邱牧師和他們的助理，受主差遣，為亞城華人基督教會的拉比；他們滿懷恩賜和愛心，是基督在亞城華人教會復興的磐石中的磐石。

關島華人基督教會於九○年代初興起，耶和華神也在這裡撒播種子，差來拉比；亞城華人基督教會的亮光，在前面照耀。關島所有信奉創造天地、自有、永有、昔在、今在、永在、萬世不變、三位一體耶和華真神的弟兄姊妹，要恆切禱告，求主憐憫，賜下愛心，讓大家謙卑、忍讓、寬恕、包容，背起主耶穌流血捨命的十字架，不分宗派、不分彼此，同心合一，同聲傳揚主耶穌的真道，使基督的福音，分享眾多的關島華人；也使關島華人基督教會大大復興。

給喬州亞城弟兄姐妹的信

亞城華人基督教會主內年長、年輕的弟兄姊妹好。蒙主恩典，並託福弟兄姐妹，我和內人來了關島，一切平安。弟兄姐妹的來信，一一收到，知道大家近況，甚為欣慰；萬里和麗仙，遠去佛州，心中十分懷念。

到了關島以後，我們參加了這裡的華人教會，忘羊回群，重享天父慈愛，和主內弟兄姊妹的關懷，使我們恢復生活的力量和行路的亮光。關島全面積小於亞城，總人口約十四萬。中國同胞，原來只有二千餘人，最近已增至五千上下。關島華人教會，仍在萌芽時期，每週禮拜，約有兄弟姐妹和慕道朋友三、四十人；情況相當於一九七〇年代、亞城華人教會搬離喬工學生活動中心、借用第十街教堂前後的查經班。這裡，每月原先僅查經和唱詩各聚會一次，最近有主內僕人唐崇平牧師、來關為主作工三個月，開始每週崇拜、查經、和證道。

亞城教會，蒙主引導，在喬工查經班時期，有多位賦有特別恩賜的弟兄，帶領讀經、禱告、和靈修，長進迅速；以後北遷，增加數位有恩賜的年輕弟兄，加上主僕陳牧師主持講壇，奠定根基，很快興旺。關

81

島華人教會，仍在創始，千頭萬緒，一切有賴主的引導，唐牧師到期回臺，講壇有待主的安排，願兄弟姐妹禱告紀念。

關島雖小，但有神斧天工的風景，為開創天地的上帝賦予人間度假的天堂。熱帶椰子樹林，高插雲天，四面環繞海洋，到處都是白沙海灘，海浪平靜輕柔。我們有時漫步海邊，舉目四望，浩瀚海洋，無邊無際。這時恍然省悟，我們都是約拿，違背了神的旨意，陷身於鯨魚腹中。也明瞭神的安排，讓我們漂流孤島，得以安靜思想，全心全意，禱告祈求。但願神施恩典，早日讓鯨魚把我們帶往尼尼微岸邊，請弟兄姊妹代禱。

掙扎於鯨魚腹中，思想起教徒的名稱。聖經新約中，有門徒、聖徒，和使徒等；主耶穌受難以前，跟從祂的，都是耶穌的門徒；安提阿教會開始，門徒稱為基督徒。今天受浸重生而歸主的弟兄姊妹，一般稱他們為教徒或信徒。所謂信徒，顧名思義，是信奉耶穌基督的教徒，以字面解說，很簡單，其實成為一個真真實實的信徒，並不容易。使徒是耶穌親自揀選，賦予特殊恩賜和異能，長於傳佈神的真道、趕鬼、醫病、說方言、帶領世人歸主的門徒，像彼得、約翰、馬太等。

　　門徒、聖徒，或信徒，因時代或語言傳譯而異，不同稱呼，無關輕重，重要在於每個信徒在十字架道路上的造就。一般而言，信主的道路，由揀選、慕道、認罪、蒙恩，一步一腳印，走向十字架。很多教徒，受了洗，天堂左卷在握，便少讀經禱告，繼續靈修，追求靈命的成長，而達到十字架的頂端。這種初信、缺乏根基的教徒，遇風遇浪，碰到試探，便會失散跌倒，無所始終。

　　舊約時代的亞伯拉罕和摩西，新約時代追隨、摸拜、和祈求耶穌醫治病患的大眾，以及與主同釘十架的犯人，都是真實的基督徒。他們有十足的信心，篤信上帝，是拯救世人、大能獨一的真神。所以亞伯拉罕老年得子，後代子孫興旺；摩西帶領以色列百姓出埃及，在曠野四十年，天降嗎哪，堅硬的磐石，流出清泉；以色列人逃離埃及，追兵緊緊逼至，窮途末路，紅海開出一條生路；長大痲瘋和血漏婦女，絕症得以醫治；與主同訂十字架的犯人，罪得赦免，而獲拯救。許多事物，世人認為不可能；上帝創造世界，主宰萬物，萬事都能，其中關鍵，在於認罪悔改，信靠真神。

　　跟隨摩西出埃及的眾多以色列人，都是耶和華的選民，卻是云云眾生，沒有確實的信心，稍遇艱困，便不能忍受；出言不遜，抱怨耶和華，不管將來的迦南美地，沉耽於昔日埃及為奴的生活。今天教會的信眾，包括我們自己，各存世俗利害，都是出埃及的以色列眾民。其中有猶大，雖是使徒，卻利慾薰心，出賣耶穌；也有彼得，面對耶穌，信誓旦旦，忠心耿耿，臨遇危險，信心動搖，含含糊糊，不認主耶穌。

保羅有羅馬公民身份，是奉主旨意而蒙呼召的使徒。蒙恩以前，他受有猶太大祭司的權柄，逼迫耶穌，殘害教徒；在大馬色的路上，受主大光照耀，皈依耶穌，為主傳道，歷經折磨。彼得為漁夫，性格單純，是耶穌第一個揀選的使徒；在跟隨主耶穌的路途中，軟弱跌倒，醒悟以後，懺悔流淚，此後歷盡艱辛，為主作工。保羅和彼得，都是世俗罪人，重生悔改以後，捨命傳道，為主殉難；因而使得耶穌基督，大大興起，傳佈萬邦。

根據記載，彼得殉道時，謙卑要求，倒釘十字架；他說世人不配，不能和主並列，同樣正釘十架。後世欽仰，保羅和彼得，都成為聖者；他們的信仰、事奉，和義行，也為主內僕人和信徒，樹立了光亮的標桿。

摩西時代，以色列人必須藉著律法，勤慎修行，一步步接近耶和華。神子降世後，耶穌以三位一體的形像，架構了神人之間的橋樑；祂降生人間馬槽，背負十字架，走向永恆的天堂。十字架的寶血，洗清世人的罪，使我們可以蒙恩得救；因此，緊緊跟隨耶穌的腳步，我們都可走向永生神的國度。一般教徒和真實信徒之間，若有區隔，只是五十步與百步，可遠可近；懺悔認罪，仰望十字架，須臾不離，大家都可以成為十足的信徒。

　　主內年長和年輕的弟兄姐妹，在主十字架的道路上，你們已經走得很深很遠，但願你們百尺竿頭，再進一步，我們追隨在後，努力向前跟進。願主同在，大家平安。

只以他人為目的，不以他人為手段。

—— 傅佩榮

趙校長

在美國南方的中國同胞，不論新到或久居，大概都知道趙校長。他不是駐美代表、僑領，或大牌教授；也不是有錢老板，或電影小生。他像你像我，黃皮膚、黑眼珠，也是芸芸眾生。

十六、七年之前，和朋友磨牙，開始聽到趙校長。當時南美同胞不多，沒有中文學校，紐約市、芝加哥等大城市，倒有一些由家長自辦、自稱的中文小學。筆者心想這位趙校長，大概是其中一個學校的自封校長，過耳便罷。

某冬，亞城為寒流籠罩，氣溫減至冰點上下，冷風刺骨。為了溫飽，筆者一如往常。起早摸黑，開著老爺車趕去上班。一路車來車往，倒不寂寞，但當此寒冬時節，邊遠郊外，行人卻是絕無僅有。

開著開著，前方不遠處，出現一位走路仁兄，頭戴防風帽，跌跌撞撞，似跑非跑，似走非走。大概同是五斗之徒，急著趕搭公車上班。回憶不久之前，在紐約北部當學生時，大風大雪之下，受好人幫助，常搭便車，省去不少風寒之苦。回報機會擺在眼前，筆者把車停了下來，行人上了車，脫了風帽，竟是一位中國老胞。

「貴姓？」

「曹ｘｘ。」

「那裏發財？」

「領事館裏幫忙。」

「嘿嘿，賓字車呢？」

「哈、哈……。」

外面風聲呼呼，車裏雜音大，我們又是王黃不分，南腔北調，雖然同說中國話，卻沒有交通很多。好在嘻嘻哈哈，事不關痛癢。印象中，曹君操江南口音，年輕朋友，四十歲上下；整齊的小平頭，露出些許少年白，中等身材。但三〇年代的西服，緊裏身上，顯得略為瘦小一些。

不久，與一群朋友趕去佛州勞德代堡，參加中華隊的少棒大賽。進了球賽場地，抬眼四望，只見新僑老僑、小學生和大教授，混坐一起，吱吱喳喳，滿場興奮。俺、儂、格、吊、宰莫宰羊，一片鄉音；有聽沒有聽，覺得份外親切。坐猶未定，看到中華小將的聚集地，一位年輕朋友，跑東跑西，整齊小平頭，一件白襯衣，一眼認出，他就是搭過筆者便車，在領事館幫忙的曹君。

棒賽開始。

「中華隊！」

「加油！」

一陣陣吶喊，有節奏，有力量，聲浪蓋滿了廣大的球場，中華兒女的血液在奔騰，黃帝子孫的熱淚湧成了巨流。在白人世界裏，被壓迫、被歧視，前代的中華移民，曾被強迫離開金山，曾被排擠於工廠門外；洗衣和做飯，成了他們唯一討生的路途。今天…，三比零，中華隊贏了，中國人站起來了；小將立了大功，全場的中國同胞，不論男女老少，不管來自天南地北，本省外省，一個個興奮發狂。

「趙校長…」一位年長的前輩，要請小將吃飯。

「趙校長…」一位小女生，爭著叫喊，一定為小將著了魔。筆者也才領悟，曹君就是趙校長。

回到旅館，沒有人睡覺。一群一堆，或聚集於房間，或圍坐於邁阿密海灘。有人談球賽，活靈活現，好像大家都是英雄。有人談小將，阿狗是他姨夫的小弟，阿良是她堂嬸的外孫，如數家珍，小將無異都是他們的一家人。

有人也談趙校長。

「他像臺北聯考場外陪考的老爸。」

「送茶遞水，殷勤撫慰。」

「校長嘛，小將都是他的學生。」

「他是戰場上的一連之長，那裏需要他，他就在那裏。」

　　為了安排各州前來參加的灰狗車、邁阿密海邊的旅社、啦啦隊等等，趙校長都煞費苦心，幾天幾夜，沒有安枕。

　　卡特背棄中華民國，老鄧趾高氣揚，加了三寸鞋底訪美。海外的中國同胞，義憤填膺，紛起抗議。美南的華僑和留學生，老老少少，集千人之眾，曾到卡特家鄉和鄧矮子所到之處，盛大遊行，由吳奶奶領軍，走在行列的最前端。吳奶奶時已八五高齡，白髮班班。許多老美朋友，眼見其情其景，也參加了遊行抗議。趙校長無愧為校長，兵危勢急，善動後勤，請出高堂岳母助陣，贏取了眾多的正義之聲。

　　鐵幕開啟之後，大陸出來了一群留學生，大致四十歲左右，都是權勢在手的新貴；不然，他們不會被放到美帝資本主義的國土；出來了，也不會回去。他們也談趙校長。

　　「昨天，他請吃飯，送我一轉一響。」

　　「他是國民黨派出來的。」

　　「他把毛主席和江青的底細，摸得很清楚。」

　　「他也去救世軍買東西。」

　　以後，筆者和趙校長混熟了，成了他的食客和聽眾。逢年過節，他總會來電話，邀請吃飯和聊天。

每去，總會碰到許多朋友，有時數十，有時成百，師嫂帶頭，大家包餃子，或煮麵條，男男女女，老老少少，大鍋造飯，歡樂一團。

每逢這樣的場合，趙校長好像又登上了升旗臺。一堆博士、碩士、教授，和年輕的留學生，都成了臺下的聽眾。打開話匣子，他上談史記、劉關張、文天祥，和史可法，忠孝節義，滔滔不絕。

「當今世代渾濁，楚河漢界不分，蘇武復生，誰會理解他的節；董孤再世，最多爬方格，三生五世，也無望於臺北市的一寸高樓。」一個年輕後生，插了一嘴。

趙校長呵呵一笑，改談毛澤東千萬人頭落地，和華國峰和鄧小平的血腥鬥爭。

「中國將來的路，怎樣走？」喬大社會系的高材生，將了一軍。

「揚棄共產黨，」趙校長正色相對。

「民主、自由、統一中國。」

加一杯紹興酒，趙校長的興致更濃，會重複一遍他和師嫂鵲橋會的戀愛故事。原來，趙校長二十來歲便膺重任，胸脯挺得高，蕭灑英俊，有膽識，有活力，深受門下挑李的崇敬。師嫂校花一朵，才貌雙全；校長校花，互慕互愛，終於結成連理。

關島彈丸小島，蠻夷之地，國內地圖，恐不見經傳。來了之後，變成了化外之民，因而經常想起趙校長和他的「三千」食客，大家午夜擺龍門，常不知東方發白。聽說，這裏也有中華會館，由商界經營。他們都是僑領，望重名片，忙於紅燈綠紙，芝麻小事，無暇顧及。因此每逢夫子誕辰，或歲末年終，加倍懷念師嫂的大鍋麵和大水餃，垂涎三尺，不知何時再可嘗到。

趙校長沒有名片，大家都以校長相稱，顯示一份親切和尊敬，很少人注意他的名和字。

父母可能不是想像中的十全十美，就如同子女也未必是十全十美的子女一樣，但親子之間的關係永遠是純潔的，不變的。父母的愛，像是春天的太陽，讓孩子在和煦的春風中成長；子女的孝，則像溫柔的月亮，溫暖了父母的心，使人性的光輝更聖潔。

— 晨旭

人生最重要的關係，是父母和子女的關係。任何一種
人生哲學，如果不講求這個根本的關係，便不能說是
適當的哲學，甚至不能說是哲學。

― 林語堂

人有三種：智者、平凡、庸者。

智者：掌握命運，解答命運，發掘問題，不相信冥冥
之中的安排。

庸者：盲從，無所適從，相信別人有能力解答他們的
命運。

平凡人：對命運極為相信，也有能力發掘問題，但才
智不足，無法解答命運，於是找算命先生。

人生不要太計較，去做你應做的事，而不是想做的
事，餘者就留給上天安排。

― 紫雲

石頭種樹

　　台北高樓連天，沒有空地，聽說許多市民，利用樓頂種植花木，遮蔭、美化，和培養身心之外，還生產鮮花蔬菜，以為點綴和佐餐。筆者離開台北很久，沒有親身經驗，但一生當中，曾經歷兩次石頭種樹，且摘記經過，略述連想於下。

　　八二三砲戰時，筆者為軍中兵卒，駐守於金門陽宅地區。砲戰發生以前，防衛司令官伯玉公是戰場名將，著重軍事防衛設施，更提倡造林舖路，修壩造湖，發展灌溉和遊樂，振興戰地民生事業。

　　金門全島，大部分由太武山所盤據；而太武山又由岩石所組成。為了全島普遍造林，玉公一度下令，駐守島上官兵，在太武山上下，每人挖鑿三個石洞，指定規格，每洞一立方公尺，各洞之間，相隔十公尺。戰地軍令如山，下達以後，將士用命，一如臨敵作戰。全軍挖空心思，用盡釘錘十字鎬，山頂山麓，日日夜夜，鏗鏗鑠鑠，一鼓作氣，一片熱鬧，流血流汗，拚命達成使命。

　　近聞報導，金島綠樹成蔭，有森林遊樂區，聽聞之後，欣喜非常。三十多年歲月，前人種下的樹，今天終於長成，可為後人遮蔭取涼了。史有西北左公柳

93

，今有金門伯玉林，左胡疆場建樹，將一同垂名於千古了。

左公柳見於歷史，今天的西北荒漠地區，是否還有柳絮飄花、綠楊吻春的勝景？太武山麓的蒼翠樹林，想必美麗壯觀。歷歷遊人，是否有人見林又見樹，記得一林一木，都是汗漬斑斑，一分一寸，開山鑽石，開墾種植而長成？因此，也連想起臺灣東部的發展，中橫公路沿途懸崖絕壁，名勝傳遍天下；乘興而來，隨風而去的遊客，有沒有人停下一步，為當年開路的白骨亡魂，追思憑弔一番？

數月以前，路絲颱風襲擊關島，颱風過後，筆者經歷了第二次石頭種樹。關島北部，全由珊瑚石形成，地層表面，僅略有浮土，所生植物，沒有深厚根基。路絲長裙飄過以後，許多大樹小樹，都被連根拔起，東倒西歪。庭院種植的一些灌木和籬笆樹，也被吹倒。

寶玉見殘紅落地，曾於大觀院中流淚葬花。筆者不是賈少爺，沒有那樣多情逸趣；但長時間以來，與院中一草一木，朝夕觸摸，無聲相語，在大自然之中，相擁相抱，混然成為一體。況且樹木迎風送涼，花兒嫣紫千紅，天天笑靨迎人，若說花木無情，則是我們不解花木之情，甚或人世的無情了。眼看這些樹木遭受路絲的肆虐，躺倒於大地的病塌上，呻吟呼痛，筆者也自然有動於衷，發起了寶玉愛及花木的感情。

沒有很多的閒時間，也沒有挖鑿珊瑚石地面的工具，為了扶救這些倒地傷殘的樹木，只有動腦筋，一切盡其在我。每棵樹或生或死，全賴於自然的安排，和它們各自的生存能力了。華陀治傷醫病，能做到的，不過如此而已。

經過了斟酌考慮，決定犧牲小我，成全大我，切除股枝，保全身軀。幾經決定，費盡一番工夫，剪除了許多枝丫，然後一一立起樹幹，歸回它們原來的位置，樹根周圍，加上水泥磚塊，和椰子果實，或壓或支。較高樹幹，並用繩索牽拉，或用剪下的殘枝支撐，以保持每棵樹幹的平衡，不致倒下。

每天巡視，每天看顧，三數月以後，許多扶起的樹幹，都長出了新芽，開始復原生長。其中一、二棵樹幹，經不起烈日照射，失水而枯乾。奇妙的是，一些用於支撐的枝丫和壓根的椰子果實，卻發芽生長，欣欣向榮。再看籬笆旁邊，一些剪下來丟棄的枝丫，也偷偷地長出綠芽，抬起了頭，和得寵的主幹樹木，競爭生長。

人們自稱為萬物之靈，常為世事立計劃，為自己立志願，為子孫而計算；但是日光之下，能立志行事，由得自己的，有幾許人？筆者生長於窮鄉僻野，避秦逃亂，走金廈而臺灣，遠遊美國南北，再轉關島，隨風飄泊，逐水草而遷；由丘八轉丘九，數次死裡逃生，一切都是意料之外的事。筆者石頭種樹，親眼看到自然界的力量；自身的生命歷程，也印証了冥冥之中，主宰的支使和安排。世事如是，所以眼看烏衣巷裡起高樓，眼看它樓塌了；皇帝公卿，雖擁有世界，皇子皇孫，亦會恨莫生於宮庭世家。放眼山外，看過地平線，我們都可心安理得，橫梁春夢，一覺睡到明天。

海 外 升 旗

　　星期五下午近七點了，仍在忙於案牘，關島大學農學院李院長來了電話，通知第二天有升旗典禮。

　　「怎麼回事？」

　　「明天是教師節，中華總會舉辦升旗、健行、和祭孔活動。」

　　「八點半在中華學校集合。」

　　李院長嘉義人，台大高材生，威斯康辛拿了農藝博士以後，便來關大任教，和協助太平洋地區推廣農業；望重學術界，為關大校長好朋友；不愧為教頭，也是關島中華總會的馬首。接到他的電話，甚為興奮欣喜。

　　星期六微曦起床，牽牽手趕去了中華學校，許多鄉親已經先到，東一群，西一堆，閩南滬粵，南腔北調，吱吱喳喳，喜氣洋洋。中華學校的大小朋友，園裡園外，跑進跑出，忙著準備。總領事、僑委、僑領陸續來到。

　　「升旗典禮開始。」小朋友，大朋友，男生和女生，有隊無伍，面對旗桿，肅穆無聲。湊完國歌，一面青天白日滿地紅的國旗，引領美國和關島旗，開始升上旗桿。在「山川壯麗，物產豐富」的抑揚音樂聲中，面對冉冉上升的國旗，熱淚盈眶，眼前一片模糊。

飄泊海外二十多年，第一次參加升旗。抬頭仰望國旗艷麗的顏色，也看到了革命、抗日、戡亂歷歷戰役中，千千萬萬先賢先烈的鮮血；往事如煙，同時想起與國旗相親相近的一、二往昔舊事。

三十多年以前，在鳳山入伍學兵時，每晨每昏，升旗降旗，是隆重大事。早上矇矓起床，晨操和越野跑步以後，一、二總隊、預訓班、留美班，數千精壯健兒，齊集司令台前，嚴肅地升起了國旗。下午夕陽西斜。數千男兒好漢，又齊集司令台前，立正稍息，單兵、班、排教練，齊步、跑步、和正步，分裂式和閱兵，然後集中，一隊一伍，一行一列，方方正正，壯重降下國旗。鋼鐵的訓練，訓練鋼鐵的隊伍。校長學兵，每時每刻，面對「主義、領袖、國家、責任、榮譽」，一心一德，盼望把青天白日滿地紅的國旗，帶回南京、北平，和全中國的土地。

數年以前，卡特背盟，筆者攜妻帶小，參與眾多同胞，高舉國旗，到卡特家鄉遊行，大旗小旗，老中老外，一片旗海，「梅花、梅花」不斷，表示嚴重抗議。時至今日，犬子的斗室之中，仍然懸掛著當年抗議使用的大小國旗，淚漬斑斑，留有海外中華兒女的憤怒和感情。

升旗畢，開始健行，目標為孔子公園，距中華學校約二、三公里。校長押隊，僑胞同鄉、學生和家長，前前後後，邊走邊蓋。國語、台語、廣東話、上海腔，興高彩烈，一片融和。半途之中，一位十三、四歲男生，開口攀談，筆者隨口應答，一來一往，說了洋文。

「和中國人，說中國話。」後面一位六、七歲小女生，搶前兩步，糾正訓斥一番。小女生是一年班的學生，一口標準國語，說話和勇氣，十足表現了中華學校的成績，也證明了中華文化，能於普天之下，薪火相傳，綿延不絕的道理。

一些流美朋友，踏上了新大陸，日常家庭生活，和自己的子女，都以洋文交談，大概急於應用惡補學到的功夫，或是望子成龍，望女成鳳，巴不得子女洋化，好和洋人爭霸天下。近聞國內有兒童英文補習班，一如往年的黃梅調，街頭巷尾，非常流行。同是天下父母心，大概也是準備子女移民歸化。

時間飛逝，轉眼十餘年，兒子帶回洋婆子，女兒跟著藍眼珠跑，男男女女，不男不女，新的世界，新的道德；見面一聲 hi，失去鄉音，不說中國話，談的不是洋足球，就是美國花邊；父母目瞪口呆，不知後生小子，亂蓋什麼；目無尊長，叫父叫母，稱名道姓；父母夫子之心，開始納悶，嘆世道式微，兒女不孝不順，沒有天倫樂趣。

一些朋友，與洋人結婚，或者父母歸化為洋，自己是第二、三代華人，完全失去鄉音，卻想盡方法，在海角天隅，支持創辦中華學校，教育子女，或把子女送回國內，接受國民教育，希望下一代能說中國話，承受四維八德，不失為龍的傳人。

月亮有圓有缺，天下事，有得必有失，學西學中，熟重熟輕，天下父母，得費苦心，作一番選擇。田長霖脫穎而出，統領柏克萊，李遠哲窮研化學，得諾貝爾獎，他們都沒有忘記方塊文字，與中國同鄉相聚，也不會陌生。國內有位名將軍，人稱哈營長，生於廣東，長於東北，青少留美，精通中英文，曾輔佐元戎，為國家有重大貢獻。前人典範，或可作為後世父母，參考借鏡。

健行到了孔子公園，大伙聚集於夫子石像面前，由中華民國駐關島的父母官，介紹夫子生平、教訓，和孝道，然後行三鞠躬禮。一陣傾盆大雨，每個人濕透衣服，分外興奮刺激，沒有絲毫咆怨。雨中散步，大大小小，又健行回中華學校，一頓包子春捲，大快朵頤之後，已是午後三點。

半字謠

——斤酒山人

半自忘形半自醉，半倒半歪舉大盃，
半半痴迷半半傻，半訴半笑半半啼。
半齊不整無小節，半生散淡了無期，
新歌老戲各半唱，清風半袖袖漸肥。
半桶清水半知解，半作工來半作詩，
半枝禿筆寫山水，半枝禿筆寫別離。
半斤米飯半天飽，半包煙卷半天吹，
半怕酸來半怕苦，半喜辣來半喜甜。
為人不會半裝笑，不敢妄自半欺言，
何苦哈腰半垂首，懷抱琵琶半遮顏。
半世韶光如夢過，未得消遙半日閑，
半煙半酒隨歌舞，半似懵懂半似癲。

陸軍官校，五十年想思

不久之前，臺灣多媒體語言教育學會召開國際研討會，地點在鳳山陸軍官校，逃兵近半個世紀，有機會回去看看母校，心中有說不出的欣喜。往事如煙，也浮現於眼前。

第一天，乘坐官校校車，離高市赴鳳山，出了旅店，沿途街市，似曾相識，卻是嶄新的面貌。車過衛武營，高高的圍牆，仍然圍繞營區，只是牆內外的樹木，長高了，長多了，也長得更蒼鬱、更茂盛了。營房外圍，以前空曠的荒地，現已瓊樓玉宇，前面廣闊的軍用直昇機場，也是房舍連連；旁邊從高屏公路通往營區的筆直大路，變成高樓腳下的小巷道；兩旁原來修剪整齊美觀的矮松行樹，經不起時間的考驗，已淘汰消失了。

以前，高魁元司令，頎長高䠷，三星掛肩，矗立在司令台，諄諄訓誨，告誡部屬，嚴守營規，勵兵抹馬。他知道官兵的口袋，欲擒固縱，曾大膽放話，要放假一個月，看看大家往那裡跑。王多年司令，短碩結實，端坐長官席，安靜平和，和軍官們分享稀飯、饅頭、花生米。張國英司令諳熟將相之道，到職第一次訓話，開宗明義，宣示做了軍團司令，已心滿意足。睽違四十多年，願長官別來無恙。

抬頭窗外，車子已過鳳山的王生明路、黃埔新村，進到了官校的側門。左側，一連三、五標語，白底紅字，極為醒目。同車來自康乃爾大學的李玉芬中文教授，看一個唸一個，唸到「不貪財」，全車來自歐美、澳紐，和其他地區的同胞，哈哈笑出了聲。今日臺灣，今日黃金世界，只有黃埔這塊乾淨的土地，不向錢看，專心愛國家、愛百姓了。

車停了，面前是中正紀念堂，歐式建築，紅頂白牆，偉宏壯觀。來到三樓會議廳，正中坐著國父中山先生的塑像，雙目炯炯，栩栩如生，後面貼身站著先總統蔣公，身著戎裝，年青英挺。塑像依據黃埔建校之初，蔣公受命擔任校長，侍奉國父時的歷史性照片複製。

民初，滿清被推翻，革命政府建立於廣州，但全國各地，軍閥割據，廣東、江浙，和奉直魯，各據一方；外有英、法、德、日、俄等，列強壓境，伺機侵奪瓜分。黃埔建校，目標為「發展革命武力，掃除革命障礙，」統一中國，抵禦外侮……黃埔建校以後，不負使命，先期師生，初試鋒芒，以五百枝步槍，打敗陳炯明，完成東征；接著清除共產黨，帶領軍民，擊潰北洋軍閥，抵定中原。抗戰軍興，黃埔師生，穿草鞋，吃五穀雜糧，團結全國同胞，以大刀和手榴彈，抵抗日本軍國強權，最後贏得勝利，廢除不平等條約，洗刷國恥，使中國擠身於世界五強。

面對國父塑像，往事歷歷，好像又回到了四十五年以前，白布汗衫，草綠軍褲，身帶汗泥，坐在三一〇教室，聆聽政治教官，娓娓講授國民革命軍史。

遙望窗外，大操場右側中央的司令台依舊，只是營區新添了許多新建築，它就今非昔比，顯得短小低矮，沒有四、五十年以前那樣壯嚴威儀了。司令台後，整齊排列著的鋼筋水泥營房，是日軍遺產，經過裝修維護，比以前更為清醒顯目。

司令台對面的設施，全部改頭換面，以前的鋁皮營房和大餐廳，已經不見。橫越大草場沿邊、官校師生的五大信念標語：主義、領袖、國家、責任、榮譽，已移了位置。這邊，現在建起了一棟新的建築，佔地似乎已沿伸到了以前緊鄰的步校營區。遙對司令台，是新的校史館，就是黃埔紀念館。五大信念，高掛正牆，一如以前，明顯醒目。

記得，司令台的號音，是全校活動的電紐，指揮師生的作息起居。每早，天色未明，司令台撥開擴音器，輕微卡擦一聲，每棟營房，每位同學，便自動驚醒，似為發條操控，跳起彈下床，衝鋒陷陣，爭十分鐘時間，解決衛生、漱洗、著裝、打綁腿，整理內務、疊豆干，然後箭般地射向集合場。號音未落，各連各隊，像水庫放閘的水，整齊快速，奔向大操場，在那裡左轉右轉，前看後對，排列組合，擺人頭方陣。晚間，息燈號響起，每位同學，又如機器人，上床倒下，沒有失眠，無顧窗前明月；偌大營區，歸於沉寂，除了風聲鼻息，餘無雜音。

司令台前的大操場，仍舊廣闊無邊。這裡，從立正、稍息，起步走，基本教練，到班排操演，每個同學，都由文弱的平民，鍛練成抬頭挺胸，頂天立地的鋼鐵軍人。這裡，每星期總有三、兩次閱兵訓練。下午夕陽西斜，各隊收操後，排列司令台對面一線，由大閱官坐車巡視，然後開始分列式，繞大操場半圈，通過司令台前，以正步向大閱官敬禮。

平常，校長為大閱官。每逢六月校慶，蔣公都要率領政府要員和高層將領，蒞校點名親校，並和師生聚餐，親自察看訓練。到了雙十節，官校學生總隊總是排列於各軍種、各部隊的前頭，雄糾糾，氣昂昂，參加總統府廣場的國慶大閱。練兵千日，用兵一時，這時官校師生，抓著機會，個個生龍活虎，用出全身功夫，全神貫注，表現常年累月的訓練；每年也贏得軍方各階層的獎勵申賀，和中外參觀佳賓的驚嘆讚賞。

中正紀念堂腳下，原是校內匐伏爬行訓練場，離地尺許，佈有鐵絲網。某日五時過後，全隊同學，全付武裝，從野外翻望雲山，越七六高地，回營行至匐伏訓練場邊，天空大雨如注，地上積水成潭，值星官於全日野外演練以後，興頭未盡，拉長馬臉，下令行動，最後三人，管理廁所三天，目標：大操場遠方的黃埔廳。從匐伏場開始，數千公尺，臥倒、起立、匐伏前進。回到營房，沒有理由，沒有鼓勵，只有滿身汗水和泥水。回憶起來，值星官當時不過官拜中尉，年富氣盛，急著要把官校傳統精神訓練的一環，傳授訓練後生而已。

校史館中，佈置了黃埔昔日的校門，不過兩邊換了聯語。時移境遷，「貪生怕死，升官發財。」大概現在已可商討斟酌了。館內佈置，甚稱完善，有黃埔、成都，和鳳山時代的官校歷史，東征、北伐、抗戰、戡亂諸役的照片。也有黃埔將領、傑出校友，和戰死沙場、成仁取義先烈的事跡，惟印像之中，似乎前者較後者更為顯著；生死有別，歷史各有見解，董孤、司馬遷幾稀？

館內另一部份展示官校現階段任務編組和學生生活。曾見大陸某些大學，也有類似展覽，其目的無非

　　提昇社會認識，以廣招來。不過這種傳統展示方式，佔據空間寬闊，編纂展出，毫無彈性，若有錄影或電子媒體處理，應更為活潑、趣味、和有效。

　　政府遷臺，蔣公於三十九年三月一日復職視事、陸軍官校也同時於鳳山復校；初期，羅友倫和謝肇齊將軍先後為校長。羅謝和當時陸軍總司令孫立人將軍同好，慣著畢挺馬褲、雪亮長靴，顯得格外神氣威嚴。羅校長南方身材，有德國軍人氣概，美軍將領風彩，操場、靶場、野外，無所不至，無所不在；學生一粒鈕扣，一個踏步，稍有不正，唯隊長是問；但從不苛責，顯出權威，也有關懷。謝校長留英，經常面容嚴肅，不善辭令；出任校長前，為教育長，是羅校長左右臂，後主持官校改制，除軍事訓練之外，加授學生學士學位。羅謝均為傑出將才，離開官校之後，並非十分如意。據說，羅校長才氣縱橫，拘泥軍中倫理，以致軍人事業，未登頂峰；謝校長本為太子太傅，卻因疏失，每況愈下，曾以譯事糊口。

　　第一總隊長，已忘其姓氏，天生軍人素質，聲音宏亮，頭腦清醒，調動大部隊，有條不紊，動作敏捷，下達命令，聲震山河，因此，官校或國慶閱兵大典，均擔任大閱指揮官。第二總隊長史逸中，據說留法，人如其名，溫文儒雅，同學之間，私底之下，都暗叫別號，稱他「講話」，因為每逢訓話，他總是拖長語音，不急不徐，以「講…話」開始，引起注意。兩位師長，離校之後，未知去向。

當時，官校鳳山營區，生氣蓬勃，除有學生一、二總隊外，有預備軍官訓練班，還有一期高中畢業留美學生訓練班。每逢早會和閱兵，全校師生齊集於大操場，或聽訓，或檢查，或受校，千軍「萬馬」急急集合，跑步分散，營區常是塵土滾滾，盛況空前。遇有康樂晚會，影歌星或南台名姬芭芭拉表演，全校師生，便各帶小板橙，整齊列隊，端坐於司令台前，歡呼喝彩。

記得，學生總隊與預訓班之間，曾因官校先來後到的傳統，舉手相互敬禮小節，暗有不同意見。今天，多少人已為公卿大夫，主持軍國大事，多少人已白髮班班，解甲歸田，回朔往事，或將汗顏不已。

媒體教育學會會議三天，再度回到廣闊壯麗、人傑地靈的鳳山陸軍官校營區，觸景生情，往事歷歷，不禁引起五十年前的想思。茲塗七言一首，以頌母校，並結束本文：

陸軍官校頌

　　怒潮激盪山河殤，青天白日匯珠江；

　　東征北伐戮朱毛，平冠雪恥登五強；

　　前仆後繼黃埔魂，繼往開來好榜樣；

　　萬里江山待從頭，瀛洲多士看臺陽。

作者慈母遺像

作者家人合照：後左起楙兒、（孫）謝恩、
　　　　　　愚兒、前中（孫）謝凡

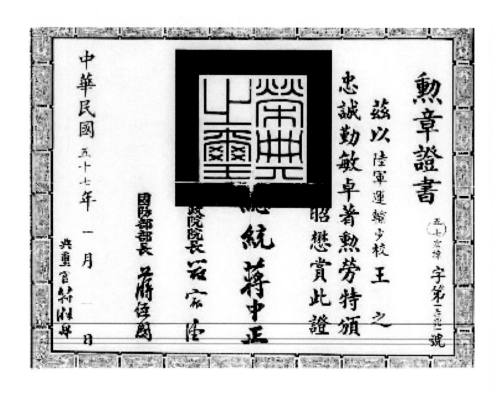

勳章證書

兹以 陸軍運輸少校 王 之

忠誠勤敏卓著勳勞特頒

昭懋賞此證

總統 蔣中正

行政院院長 嚴家淦

國防部部長 蔣經國

典重官 羅列坤

中華民國 五十七年 一月 一 日

(五十六年) 字第一三九二號

112

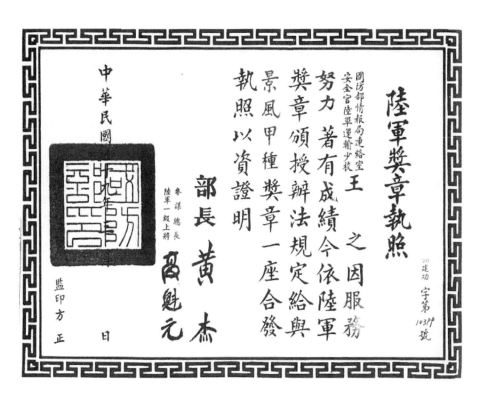

陸軍獎章執照

貳建功 字第 103/9 號

國防部情報局連絡室
安全官陸軍運輸少校 王 之 因服務
努力著有成績令依陸軍
獎章頒授辦法規定給與
景風甲種獎章一座合發
執照以資證明

部長 黃杰

參謀總長
陸軍一級上將 召魁元

中華民國

監印 方 正

日

113

陸軍獎章執照

（登）寶三字第　號

陸軍少校王　之因服務
勤奮著有成績今依陸軍
獎章頒授辦法規定給與
三星寶星獎章一座合發
執照以資證明

國防部部長　人俞大維

參謀總長　彭孟緝

中華民國　　　年　月　三　日

監印方正

114

勳、獎、紀念章

說東話西談東西
—外國人的中、英文

　　不久之前，「中副」常有小仲小品，談英文單字短辭，不但有助學習英文，且饒有趣味，每篇必讀，每讀也想回應，只是墨汁不多，沒有提筆。近讀《中央日報》網路論壇，有楊老師談如何寫英文地址，文尾標舉一例，作為結束。惟所舉之例，一點之餘，也有商確處，因而引起連想，藉此說東話西，談談外國人書寫和修讀中英文的軼事。野叟獻曝，或可為茶餘飯後的談趣，緩和 SARS 帶來的緊張，減少恐慌。

　　以前在校念書時，曾選英文寫作錯誤研究。老師每課發下一、二頁前人大作，要求研讀，找出錯失，予以改正，下堂提出討論，求善求美。所選教材，有拼字、文法、句子結構等問題；有洋涇濱創作，如 long time no see、people mountain people sea、like fire like tea。妙句如珠，笑話連連。

　　SARS 初侵臺灣，一般人輕鬆自若，笑說不喝沙士，便沒事了。SARS 連及沙士，與前面的創作，異文同工。只是 long time no see 由美國大兵傳開，現已見怪不怪，無所謂雅俗了；且 see、sea、tea 同韻，句文之中，更改中文，有兩個層次的創意；後者會意謬誤，大家疏忽輕心，任病毒爆發開來，以致損害慘重。雖屬苦笑話，也是隱喻，暗示語言文字誤導的後果。

鑄字弼文難為，大家難免敗筆，因此，錯別字，天下皆有，奇文怪作，俯拾皆是。坊間有彙編多冊，收集全世界英文奇妙創作，內容豐富，有取自英美大報標題，大家傑作；有政客的演講，律師的訴狀，大街巨道的廣告標語，餐館的菜單；形形色色，無所不包。外國人的英文選讀，尤其精彩。

修習語文，除了拼字、文法、句子結構以外，還牽涉語文習慣和文化背景，能夠學到得心應手，運用自如，實非容易。一點一勾，一個字母顛到差錯，差之毫釐，相去千里，意義完全不同；個別單字，連成片語，變成新的意義。標點句讀移了位置，改變了文意；下雨天、留客天，說法多端，大家熟稔。蔡元培先生書房用以自勉的「好讀書不好讀書」，加以標點，也可以變成不同意義的讀句。

且說某老伴出遊南美海島，言定先住天堂大旅館。老婆因事遲一天出發，老公打前站，搭機先行，到了目的地以後，發了一通電子信件，傳送回家。但因老眼昏花，長途飛行以後，心神未定，把電子信箱地址中的 c 打了 e，電子信息轉了位置，送到了另一位老婦人的信箱。

無巧不成書，這位老婦人適於日前喪夫，打開信箱，看到天外飛來的電子信件，眼前一黑，即刻昏倒，不省人事。回家奔喪、照顧老母的女兒，聽到了聲音，從隔室趕了過來，眼睛一瞄，看到電腦畫面的文字：「老伴，天堂佳境，美景無限好，我已報到，也已為妳登記，明天見。」

e 與 c 差不多，只是小小勾了一頂點兒，但也差不多把一位老婦人送去天堂，提早伴老伴去了。

三、四十年以前，台北車站前，漢口街一帶，英文補習班如雨後春筍，到處林立。某一托福簽證補習中心，日夜趕工，準備大拼經濟，撈一筆留學潮的留學財，門口面朝車站、人來人往的大櫥窗，張貼了兩張斗大字體的廣告，左邊中文：「即將開班」，右邊英文：「CLOSE TO OPEN。」

一九九〇年前後，上海十里洋場，又蓬勃興盛了起來，人潮擁擠的南京路，開了一家高級自助餐館，室內佈置，喜氣洋洋，大紅燈籠高高掛，上面並排寫著「Eat all you can until you are fed up」，自選盡吃，吃飽為止。

開羅郊外，有一個毛驢場，供觀光客乘騎使用，為廣招來，門前慳了一個標語 Come to ride on your own ass。

這些英文創作，已是陳年經典，好久以前的句子了，現在的台北郎、上海倪，看了也會會心一笑。托福簽證班的英文廣告，一關一開，英美洋人糊塗了。後面的 fed up，大概飽了和夠了，一念之別，說法相異；美國人指 ass（驢）為卡蔥，外人知其一，不知其二，矇在鼓裡，搞笑難免。類似俚俗英語，小仲先生研究頗深，會深入淺出，談得津津有味。

東方和非英語國家，創造了許許多多英文佳作；西方人修習中國語文，也有不少並駕齊驅，互相媲美的創作。中副曾有俞創毫先生〈如此中文〉大作，摘錄了一些美國藝術大家公開展出的創作，諸如「愛愈治都」 love heals all、「背後山」 behind the mountain、聖經譯文「聖希愛」等等語不驚人死不休的句子，乍看之下，好像日語，卻近中文，似曾相識，卻不知意何所指。

很久以前，有一則故事，述說美國長春籐名校，一位著名漢學家，教授一班洋學生，學習第二學年的中文。

「我們已經學過『東』和『西』字，」名漢學家老神在在，順手在黑板上揮了兩個大字，英語夾點中文，開腔教學。

「這兩字指示兩個相反的方向，」大部分說英語。

「這邊是『東』，那邊是『西』，」學生的眼目左顧右盼，東張西望。

「隔壁文史大樓在⋯」

「東，」學生回應。

「圖書館在⋯」

「西。」

「Very good。」

「我們在 middle，不東也不西。」學生頻頻點頭。

「我們不東不西，」名家帶領，學生大聲唱和了好幾遍。

「這兩字連在一起，」教室平靜以後，漢學家夾著英語和中文，繼續講授，「就不是東，也不是西了，而是東西，一樣東西。」丈二金剛，學生迷失了。

「桌子是『東西』，椅子是『東西』。」名家舉例解釋，「人不是『東西』。」

＊＊＊＊＊　　　　＊＊＊＊＊

「Book 是『東西』。」

「人不是『東西』。」

「你不是『東西』。」

「我不是『東西』。」

「我們都不是『東西』。」

漢學家聲音宏亮，教學經驗豐富，深諳語言教材教法，把預先準備的材料，時隱時現，一個多鐘頭，帶領學生，反反覆覆，高聲練唱，重音放在「不是東西」，特別加重語氣。

臺灣小民好可愛──
三二○返臺投票見聞點滴

「好香，好好吃，怎麼賣？」

「真好，真好，饅頭、大包，一個八元；豆漿、米漿，一杯十元；燒餅、油條⋯」

「沒有臺幣？」

「沒有關係，先選先拿，回頭有便，再拿來。」

回臺第二天早晨，白髮零亂，衣衫不整，一副外來老土，散步閑逛竹科側門早市，看到路邊的早點小吃，各色黃白雜糧饅頭，豆奶、米漿，熱騰騰，香噴噴，大動食頤。插進了來來往往的摩托車陣，三三兩兩的學生群，和早點小吃攤年輕的女老闆攀談起來。她沒有側目，絲毫沒有不耐，輕鬆利落，給了很甜的回應。

*****   *****

木柵開往榮總的欣欣專線公車，到了公館捷運站，大家都下了車。

「去那裡？」

「榮總。」

「只有你一個人了。」

「我可以搭捷運去。」

「既來之，則安之；上了車，我送你到底。」

「大選結果，真無聊，」司機打破了車中的沉靜。

「啊，啊。」不想多談，免得惹禍。

「兩顆子彈，連任了，算甚麼！」

「怎麼辦？」

「連戰有學問，有經驗，有氣度；正人君子，碰到了地痞無懶，被欺蒙，被暗算，不明不白，遭到毒手，飲恨城下，真為他叫屈。」

到了目的地，司機不厭其煩，詳細指點我，搭接駁車，轉捷運回程。「接駁車，不用付錢。」臨下車，司機又叮嚀一番。

　　＊＊＊＊＊　　　　　　＊＊＊＊＊

過了幾天，又往榮總，再次遇見了老朋友。車子到了萬芳，一位長者迷失了。司機和和氣氣，耐著性子，幫助了他。

「你的駕駛技術高明，更有十足的耐性。」車子出了社子，路況平靜了，又和司機朋友攀談了起來。

「不敢，不敢。」

「你每天面對來來往往的乘客，三教九流，無所不有，言語應對，很不容易。」

「我已開了二十多年的公車，也交了很多乘客朋友，一、二年，可以退休了。我們開公車的，開一輩車子，平平安安，全身退休，不是很多。」

很高興交了一位欣欣公車的司機朋友。

＊＊＊＊＊　　　　　＊＊＊＊＊

老婆受到感染，嚴重感冒，急急忙忙，跑去了臺大醫院，沒有身份證，沒有護照，也沒有健保卡。幸虧熱心的志工，引導她樓上樓下，東轉西轉，沒有多少功夫，見了醫生，給她取了方。醫生網開一面，給了相當的優待；結算下來，診斷和處方，費用合理。

我也利用時間，看了臺大秘尿科劉詩彬、榮總耳科廖文輝、眼科葉剛詳等醫生；也在榮總住了一天半，作全身體檢，由林俊呈等醫生主持。

我和老妻，很久沒有回臺灣，第一次到臺大和榮總醫院。世界一流的醫護設施，人才、設備，和服務，名不虛傳，令人印像深刻。各醫院內部，方向標示，清楚明白；作業流程，有條不紊；醫生、護理、技佐、和行政人員，和藹親切，年長病友，口呼伯伯叔叔。第一線志工，特別有助初來新到的病友，指示方向，省了大家東跑西撞的冤枉時間。住榮總體檢，衣食房間，無異住宿觀光旅館。

　　過去曾聞一些傳言，聽說要去臺大、榮總看病體檢，要走小道。回國前後，多方問訊，沒有得到確定的答覆，心中一直疑雲重重。親身經歷以後，發現兩個著名醫院，都可以當日掛號，當日門診。住院體檢，願意付費，一、二天內，即可受理；檢查報告，中英文並列，也於兩星期內，寄達海外。而且，網上可以登記掛號。

　　＊＊＊＊＊　　　　　　＊＊＊＊＊

　　迷失夜郎府，糊糊塗塗，摸來了四維精舍，門口一面招貼，潔白宣紙： 忠義志工茶敘。裡面好一堆人，很多長者，也有年輕人。

　　「請問先生…？」接待人員迎了上來。

　　「抱歉，誤闖地方。」

　　「歡迎進來坐，喝杯茶。」

　　「…。」

　　「沒關係，票投完了，我們歡送海外同胞，他們化錢化時間，遠從各地回來，辛苦了。我們喝喝茶，聊聊天，表示謝意，也消消鬱卒不平的心，讓大家平平安安回去。」

　　不請之客，不敢逗留。台灣心，中華情，裝滿了一背包。

＊＊＊＊＊　　　　　　　＊＊＊＊＊

「中華路的『錢櫃』。」上了計程車，交待了司機。

「唱卡拉OK？」阿港伯的鄉音。

「附近吃點心。」

「轉來投票？」

「還有其他的事，」很想避免選舉結果的高氣壓。

「沒見笑，做黑槍，臺灣之恥！」

「沒法度，」免強以生硬的臺語回答。

「我們小百姓，誰做總統都一樣…。」

「Yes!」我沒有說出口。

「那些流氓壞人還要玩四年，我們怎樣活下去？」

「唉，」叫我怎樣回應？

「我不管了，他們上我的車，我都把他們趕下去！」

＊＊＊＊＊　　　　　　　＊＊＊＊＊

「安康。」萬芳捷運站下了車，夜色蒼茫，細雨濛濛，路途不熟，隨手又攔了計程車，交待了目的地，路程不遠，司機應該熟悉。

車子朝前開去，周邊的景物不對了。「這是去新店的方向？」

「是的，要去安坑？」

「安康，興隆路四段底。」

「啊，安康社區。」

車子調轉了頭，不一回，到了目的地，碼表跳了一百五十元，司機只要八十元，我也略表大方，並深深謝了他。各自退一步，大家滿心歡喜。

多年以前，作臨時地陪，和外國朋友，一起在香港逛街血拼，九龍、新界，轉來轉去，海底隧道，過去又折返，冤枉送了不少港幣。回憶起來，臺灣小百姓，真可愛。

今上有權有勢，任意操弄，無信無義，竊取政府名器，搶奪國家財寶。計程車司機，有禮有守，不取幾十元臺幣。對比起來，臺灣同胞，臺灣的小百姓，更純真可愛。

＊＊＊＊＊　　　　　　＊＊＊＊＊

無黨派，無色彩，沒人鼓吹，沒人拉票，三二〇大選，飛回臺灣投票，只是盡點義務，心安理得，是大為高興的事。看到了政治大盜，利慾薰心，眾目睽睽之下，竟然偷天換日，無法無天，偷取大位，不禁為臺灣悲哀，為臺灣的民主嘆息！

　　進出臺大和榮總醫院，看到眾多醫護人員，兢兢業業，滿懷愛心，看護病友；成群義務志工，捨棄自我，服務社會大眾；遊逛臺灣街市，看到公車計程車司機，大家喜樂相待，誠信不欺；看到市井小民，云云眾生的血液裡，仍有中華民族古聖先賢的遺傳種子，循規蹈矩，講信修睦，則為臺灣人民慶幸，高興中華民國還有生機。

SEVEN DAYS ON GUAM

When the airplane landed at the Guam airport, my eyes began to wander around to see if someone was looking for me. While I was waiting for the baggage, I began to think about what I should do if nobody came to meet me. This was an unnecessary worry. For as soon as I approached to the exit leading to the waiting room, I spotted a poster proclaiming "HAFA ADAI" on the glass window. Along with it were additional welcome posters written in Chinese and English.

When I stepped out of the exit door, several of my professional colleagues came forward and greeted me. I was completely overwhelmed by the informal welcome, which was indeed warmer than the climate on the island. It was one of the first OOGs （Only On Guam） I learned on Guam. Since Guam is not in the West or in the East, I would call the welcome a "midway" style.

When I got out of the airport, I walked straight into a widely open world. I raised my eyes and looked toward the faraway horizon, where the beautiful blue sky was embracing the pretty, deep, and dark ocean. A few patches

of white clouds were floating by peacefully. A number of high-rise hotels stood along near the ocean's edge. I was bewildered and wondered if I was in a dream.

"This is Tumon Bay." My friend driving the car brought me back to the real world. "That is Two Lovers' Point."

Because of the variation of time, I went to bed immediately when I arrived at the apartment. "Oo-oo-wu, oo-oo-wu." The cock's crow sounded like music from a symphony. The sweet noises woke me up in the middle of the night. I do not know how many years had passed since the last time I had heard the cockcrow. I do remember it was actually the night clock in my home village. I got up and walked out into the open air. I began to count the shining stars in the sky. Ah, it could be just like my home village if there were not so many cars and shooting clubs around here.

On the next day, I began to look for a car and an apartment. I made many telephone calls. When I asked where the car was, I was usually told: "Turn right and pass the two palm trees; you will see the world's biggest McDonald's." "This is another OOG." I was told.

Everybody tells the direction to places by describing landmarks. Nobody cares about the street names and the road signs.

On the third night, I woke up at about three o'clock and could not quickly fall asleep again because of the jetlag effect. I got up and walked to the nearby beach. The noises of the day were almost gone. It seemed that the world had fallen asleep now. On the beach, I could only hear the whispers uttered by the gentle waves as they kissed the quiet land. The soft lights dotted spots here and there along the seashore.

Ah, so tender was the breeze blowing from the ocean; so sweet was the night on the beach. In time, I sat down against a palm tree and fell into a dream. A mermaid suddenly appeared. I was not sure whether she was from the ocean, the land, or the air.

She waved gently and sweetly to me and then moved swiftly toward me. She said she was there to swim while she took off her blouse in front of me without a little hesitation and threw to me her pink bras and tiny bikini. I took a deep breath and cowardly told her that for a nickel an hour, I would take care of her clothes.

Without a word, she turned around and jumped into the ocean quickly. I then fell into dream again. I did not know how long she was in the water, but when she came back, I completely forgot to charge her and let her go free.

Taking a walk has been one of my regular habits. Since arriving in Tumon, I have taken a walk every morning and evening. Before the sunrise and after the sunset, barefooted with only a bathing suit, taking a walk along the beach to Two Lovers' Point and to Ypao Park is an extraordinary experience.

Sometimes I splashed into the water trying to talk to fishes. Very often, I would not see many of them. Occasionally, 1 would run for a few minutes. But 1 always kept my own pace with no intention of competing or colliding with others along the beach.

The deserted strongholds along the seashore brought back my memory. Many years ago, I was stationed in one of such concrete forts fighting for a special cause. One day I wandered into one of the strongholds, thinking that I might find a tiny trace revealing who had fought in it. It was all in vain. Where are those heroes now? Are their bodies and souls still buried deep in the beach?

When it was raining, I usually took an umbrella with me. It was particularly interesting to walk in the rain as it moves across the ocean and over the white sand. However, when walking in the rain, I always wondered why I would need an umbrella over my head. My natural skin should be waterproof. Actually, I wore nothing that could be wet by the rain.

During such a time, I would realize why Chamorros did not wear the modern clothes in the early days. The palm leaves were sufficient enough to serve the needs of the

people on the island. I then became suspicious about the meaning of the Western civilization to the island people. Did it only bring to the people superficiality, complication, and sophistication at the cost of simplicity, purity, and honesty? Would the beach be much cleaner and more beautiful if the modern world had not brought empty cans, bottles, and other "civilized" trashes to the island?

翠死因毛貴，龜亡為殼靈，
不如無用物，安樂過此生。

　　　　　　　　　— 朱熹

THE JOYS AND VICISSITUDES OF ENFIELD

One year ago, when I came to interview for a job, I was asked why I was interested in coming to Enfield. If I were diplomatic, I would have said that "people are handsome, the weather is mild, and the landscape is beautiful here," which is indeed true about Enfield. Instead, I responded that I liked working in a small town, where people could have human touches. And this was a town in New England, which was the cradle of civilization in the New World. I was offered the job, since no Indian was in the interview team and the Indian Museum is on the remote mountaintop.

Now, I am back in the Sunbelt. However, during many deep and dark nights, my mind wandered back to the fresh air enveloping Somers' mountains, the cool and comfortable seasons in New England, and the friendly people in and around Enfield. My years in Enfield were indeed very rich, wonderful and memorable.

I was particularly impressed by the dedication and the courtesy of the Enfield police. They promptly responded

to my emergency call when I was robbed at a motel in my first night in Enfield. They fought a real battle with the robber, who was armed, though he escaped. They are law enforcers, but they, too, are human brothers. I had two traffic incidents during the first year in Enfield. I can recall some details of the incidents and my conversation with police brothers. Both times, they only warned me what I was wrong but did not issue me tickets. I was excused because I was a newcomer in the town. While many cops in other places might be corrupt, it is very fortunate that Enfield has honest and helpful cops.

The clerks and the judges in the Enfield Superior Court are special people. When I went to them seeking compensation for my loss in a robbery that occurred in a hotel earlier, they extended their hands and suggested the course I should take. The final and fair decision, made by the judge, especially healed my wound. The decision also convinced me the beauty and the justice of laws. In the court case, I was only a helpless individual against a giant corporation with a defence attorney.

Housing in and around Enfield was another side of the story. I cannot recall how many calls and visits I had made in order to rent a dwelling place during the first week in my new job. Very often, I could only talk to a machine; and I would not even receive a return call. I filled out quite a few leasing applications, which were probably turned into trashcans even before I stepped out of the rental offices.

Many landlords were perhaps richer than John B. Connall when he was the governor of Texas. Once I talked to a landlord over the telephone. Only after exchanging a few words, she began to threaten me that she would throw me out.

In the past year when I was in Enfield, I personally saw the helplessness of being thrown out of the dwelling place. I still remember the newspaper ads about property value in the Enfield vicinity, which, to me, was much higher than that of 1970's gas wells. A hare room was asking for "$120 a week," with no visitors allowed in the paid room of the tenant.

Civilization improves the living standards of human beings. Civilization may also allure humans to becoming greedier and greedier. Once I came hack from a supermarket and found that I had been charged for an item

not in my shopping bag. The difference was only a few dollars. I could only amuse myself that the young teens were really smart with cash registers. The rumour was that this was not an accident, but was a practice that would serve the greed of the business owner.

Another time, I tried to take advantage of a sale in a department store. The store's advertisement offered one-third off the regular price, including a factory rebate, for an item of its merchandise. I drove to the store and bought a couple of those items. However, the store had no rebate coupon, and two hours of my time were wasted. Shoplifting is a crime. But ripping off shoppers bas always been excused as a normal error. It is an interesting world.

Sayonara, Enfield; I miss you. Between the shadows of the high-rises of Boston and New York, I wish you would always be Enfield, a lovely town with natural beauty, simplicity and honesty.

OPEN HOUSE AT THE SNOW WHITE COLLEGE

After fifteen years being out of school, my friend Kay started college at the Snow White about two months ago. She was excited and kept calling me about many good things at the college. A few weeks ago, she insisted that I had to come to the Open House day to see the College. Having been living in the Blue Ridge Hill for my whole life, I was hesitated to come to New England, the nurturing land of liberal rebels.

"We have an English instructor graduated from Yale." Kay told me proudly when we were on the way to the Snow White College on the Open House day. She then spoke loudly about the drama club, the ski club....

"Watch your wheel." I reminded her to drive carefully. "Do your school try to recruit minority faculty and students as many other colleges are doing?"

"I heard they're talking about that, but...." She murmured.

When entering the front gate, Kay showed me with all her pleasure the photos of the faculty and staff arranged

on the wall.

"Mikie, a janitor; Liz, a kitchen help..." Kay pointed one after another at the photos. Their 4 x 6 inch smiling pictures were posted in the top middle.

"Who is your president?" I inquired curiously. "I don't know if we have a president."

Kay looked on the exhibition wall for a while and then pointed to a picture of Afro male about 1 x 1 inch at the bottom.

"He may be the one. They call him N--."

"What?"

"They also call him I--"

"Irony?"

"Oh, may be."

Although I did not like the touch of hue on the border of the photo exhibition, I liked the overall design and arrangement of the exhibition wall. It displayed the principle of simplicity, purity, and unity; and extended the meaning of the school's name. A job well done! I thank to my fellow gatekeepers.

Kay took me walking around and we enjoyed many great events. Balloons were flying over all campus.

Children were having face-painted in the cafeteria. I was disappointed, however, that balloons were all colored. And I really did not like the idea of painting kids' faces, be it black, brown, or red.

不會說笑話的人說笑話，常鬧笑話；
不說實話的人說實話，不像實話。
被人騙了，表示你忠厚，
被人騙了錢，你不但忠厚，還比他富有。
— 老 康

"SAVE MY MOM," GRACE WEPT

Grace Chung, 11, was one of the 226 victims of the Korean Airline, KAL 801 crash on August 6. Her mother Gloria; brother, Timothy; sister, Lynda; and brother in law, Ben Hsu were all killed in the crash.

Grace, the youngest of the Chung family, was one of the original 29 survivors in the crash. She was first listed under critical condition in the Naval Hospital; flew to the Brooke Army Medical Center in San Antonio, Texas; and passed away on August 10. She was cremated; her ash was brought back to Guam, and is now waiting to be buried with her family when their bodies are identified.

"Save my mom," Grace murmured with tears in her eyes when she was found among the crushed bodies and in the burning debris. Half of her face and body were burnt.

"Tim, Lin....? Are you...?" Grace whispered even though she was weak and exhausted. Her rescuers reported.

"I'm O.K." She told her auntie, Hsao-ming Hsu, the first of her relatives who visited Grace in the hospital in the Wednesday morning after the devastating crash.

"Grands here?" She moved her eyeballs and her tears were hanging on her small brown face.

"I am going to send you back to the states."

"I haven't seen the ocean."

"Come back later."

"Yea, when Lin graduates from high school next year." She chatted with her doctor in the next morning.

The Chungs were the devoted members of the Atlanta Chinese Christian Church. They were coming to visit Grace's grand parents, auntie, and uncles, who have been running business on Guam. Kai-yin, Grace father, was supposed to join his family a few days later. They haven't

seen their relatives on Guam for seven or eight years. It would have been a hilarious family reunion.

　平常心很難假裝。內心一在乎，形貌就婉媚；內心一畏懼，形貌就傴僂；內心一忿怒，形貌就剛愎；內心一憂愁，形貌就皺蹙。只有平常心的人，不震怖，不慌亂，言辭溫和，形貌才安閑。

　好勝者必爭，貪榮者必辱，淡一些才能自得其樂，不嫉妒別人，才使自己得到許多安寧。淡一些才能謹守本分，聞讚譽而喜就嫌躁，聞毀謗而怒就嫌暴。懂得守本分的人，才有資格說平常心。到了一切不假外求，才能自我滿足，忘懷得失。

　　　　　　　　　　　　　　　　　　——黃永武

J & J

Jupiter was an over six feet tall and slender Caucasian, 38 years old, and teaching English at Florida State University. He was discomfited and grasped that he would have discommodity to be tenured in the next two years. Obviously, he had not come up with improvised works seen in refereed journals. Worse, he had imprudently and impudently impugned his department chair, demurring her ill-bred and ill-disposed manners.

After evaluating several vademecums for job-hunting, over one year of searches, and intensive interviews, he was proposed the position of an associate professor by Xiver University on Taotau, a tropic island in the Southern Pacific. He impromptu accepted the proposal, evicted himself from FSU in May, and vagabondized improvidently to the island, leaving his lovely wife and two sweet teenage daughters in their Florida home.

A wave of warm, humid, and sticky air seized him as soon as Jupiter stepped out of the plane on Taotau. With the tie loosely hanging on his neck, sleeves rolled up, and everted jacket in his left arm, he took a deep breath

managing to cope with the new atmosphere; still his sweat was flowing from his face and his shirt was soaked. Propitiously, his mentor from Xiver met him at the exit of the customs and soon he was taken to a tolerable apartment in Yayoo Inlet.

After several days of bustling and hustling on campus, Jupiter still had not tuned himself to the Pacific Time. One night, he woke up and could not fall asleep again, and it was only two o'clock. With a swimming short and a slipper, he limped and stumbled to a nearby beach, and sat on the wet and soft sands with his back against a tall palm tree. The breeze gently touched the land; a sea of stars over the high vault were blinking and winking. Soon, Jupiter's eyelids were forced down.

"Excuse me, sir," the voice was sweeter and tender than the aura of the zephyr in his dream. Jupiter was trembled, confused, and fainted at the moment.

"Yes, honey." He involuntarily opened his eyes and spontaneously responded. Under the slight moonlight and one or two feet away, standing there were, like bamboo shoots of the spring, two tall, straight, and fair legs, on the top of which mounted the salient triangle junction, veiled

146

only by the shade of a dangling palm leaf.

"Please help me take a picture." Jupiter was still puzzling and wondering if she was a mermaid or her sweet wife, the angel enchanted him again.

"Yes, mom," Jupiter turned around and stood up impulsively. She handed over her Canon, swung back a few steps, and posted herself at the edge of the ocean.

Jupiter raised the Canon and stared, through the camera window, at the striking tall and well-developed body closely in front of his eye. Her two round breasts in a tight and tiny two-piece bikini, protruding out like two high mounts and pounding the heart and debilitated the feet of Jupiter. He was almost anaesthetised then and there.

As a peacock caring for her splendid fur, the angel raised her delicate hands at times in an effort to settle down her gorgeous shoulder-length hair, which was dancing and tossing with the mild wind, that also enticed Jupiter, roaming into an inviting dreamland.

"I am June." Having had a few snapshots with flashlights, they sat down side by side on the sands under the palm. Jupiter learned that June was 27, an

amalgam of Chinese and Portuguese. The beach was quiet and cool; the moonlight was soft and sweet; and the spacious gulf was holding the unrest ocean attentively and compassionately.

Now, Jupiter and June both were drunk. He began whispering in her ears and rambling in her soul the lyrical verse:

And I will make thee beds of Roses,

And a thousand fragrant poesies,

A cap of flowers, and a kurtle,

Improydred all with leaues of Mirtle,

A gowne made of the finest wooll,

Which from our pretty Lambes we pull,

Fayre lined slippers for the cold,

With buckles of the purest gold.

A belt of straw and Iuie buds,

With Corall clasps and Amber studs,

And if these pleasures may thee moue,

Come liue with me, and be my loue.

The Sheepheards Swaines shall daunce & sing

For thy delight each May-morning.

If these delights thy minde may moue,

Then liue with mee, and be my loue.

Instead of the Nimphs Reply, June was muttering with tears:

Kiss me tender;

love me more;

and hold me closer,

....

The world was lost; the two wild animals kissed, rubbed, squeezed, devoured, and rolled over on the sands again and again. The moon retired and a pale hue appeared in the sky when their energy was exhausted; and their passion, demulcent. June then got up, grabbed her new lover, tendered him another prolonged kiss. She would have a Continental flight to Hong Kong at 6:30 a.m.

June was gone. Jupiter even woke up earlier now. The noises from the neighbouring shooting clubs and the nuisances of the cockcrow from the far and near villages turned higher and louder, that disturbed and irritated him more than those of the last week. With a simple swimming suit as usual, he strolled again and again to the same spot where he had had a rendezvous with his new love.

The moonshine is kissing
   the ocean wave.
The ocean wave loves
   the moonshine.
How could I, how could I
   not to think of her,
During this silvery mellow night?

There sitting under the palms, he hummed and thrummed the melody he usually sang in high school. Before long, he again fell into dreams, hugging, kissing, and caressing his angel. June and his sweet wife emerged from time to time; but quite frequently, they were merged.

It was in the first class of American Literature I. Just when students about finished introducing themselves, the angel, with her chin slightly raised and her body harmoniously balanced, bounded in, glanced at the room for a moment, and headed straight towards the front row. The lower portion of her pink skirt, which was embellished with lovelies-bleeding flowers, whirled about behind her; the crystal clack from each of her stride overwhelmed the class. Students, males and females, all turned their eyes at her.

"June--from--Macao--." Gently, firmly, and promptly she announced as soon as she took a seat. Standing in front of the class, stunned, and bewildered, Jupiter stared at her for a long while. With a slight blush but a great delight at seeing the instructor, June responded to Jupiter's gaze with a demure and gracious smile that cabled to him a thousand words of message, which mollified the anguish harboured in his heart for thinking of her day and night.

The class was rashly dismissed. Jupiter was already overpowered when June had hardly trod into his office. He embraced her into his arms, breathing from her cream body the same bouquet that conquered him at the beach, gawking at her blue dark eyes the tempting attraction that captivated him a while ago. On the floor, he anxiously and fervently kissed all over her, from her eyelids to each of her toes. June rejoined passionately while grunting unconsciously, "J--J--J--." The turmoil of their intensive tempest vibrated the small room and crushed Jupiter's family frame to the floor.

Telephone was ringing.

"...."

"J, how is your hair? Is it growing?"

"Tickets have been reserved; we'll be with you next Wednesday." It was his wife from Florida.

"Is the beach on Taotau poisoned or polluted?" His daughter asked.

"Do you have a game in your office?" His younger daughter requested.

"Kiss you, J."

"Kiss you, dad."

"See you, dad."

Jupiter now collapsed in his chair, entangling in a perplexing love net.

WANDERING IN THE LIBRARY

My heart is beating fast and my strides are becoming rapid every time when I am walking to a library. My sweat and panting after a long journey are all gone as soon as I stroll inside a library building, whether it is a stupendous or a humble one. The busy world and its mundane noises would be left behind in street when my eyes contact the thousands of books aligned on the endless shelves in the library.

Oh, here is an ocean of books, a multitude of human minds. They come from all over the world; some might have just arrived in the library a few moments ago; others might have quartered here in the tranquillity for decades or centuries. Some of them are elegantly decorated; others, plainly dressed; and still others, loftily posted. With a variety of backgrounds, characteristics, and features, they form many different groups, either assembling themselves orderly on shelves or lying themselves here and there.

Some books are blinking their perceptive eyes, looking vigilantly; pricking up their keen ears, listening attentively; and waiting patiently, ready to offer services

to the hungry needs of human minds. They are constantly aware of their charges and always prepared to provide their wisdom, ideas, or advices to nurture those barren and wandering human souls. Wise or subtle they might be, readers have their own liberty of choices.

Either respectfully standing on shelves or majestically sitting on tables, these books all have a noble goal: they are born to attend to their human friends. They devote their whole lives to help, day and night, millions of people, who come to libraries in quest of knowledge and information. Without a slight dissension and reservation, they offer to library users whatever they may need: a simple word, a short sentence, a brief paragraph, or an entire chapter, either for a quick browsing, an instantaneous comprehension, or a long-lasting appreciation.

Bulky tomes or thin pamphlets, large folios or minuscule manuscripts, leather-bound classics or humble paperbacks, in alphabets or in pictographs, and in sciences or in humanities; with different physical sizes, various means of expression, and numerous ingredients of substances, all kinds of books amass en masse, volume after volume, in the library. Like the giant Himalayas, the vast Pacific, or the boundless African wood, the massive world of innumerable books in the library stores immense resources of treasures. They are there, anxious to enrich the minds of all mankind, to solace the souls of the needy, and to lift the spirits of the masses.

Individually or in groups, men and women constantly rush or hush into libraries. No matter they are scholars seeking knowledge, students searching for information, or the public looking for entertainment, they are all questing for their specific needs. Once they are there, they will bury themselves into the mountain forgetting about day or night,

meals or drinks. When a curious classic is discovered, they will anxiously turn it open and tenderly kiss its decayed pages, therein they could smell the fragrance of the history, sense the spiritual words of the past, and even feel the frequent touches of other bibliophiles.

These men and women go to libraries with their own purposes and needs. They may be there to hunt for data, information, ideas, or novels. After exploring here and there, labouring long, long hours, and filling full their heads, baskets, or bags, they then quietly and satisfactorily step out of the door with a notion of gratification shining

on their faces.

It would be marvellous if I could turn a library into my own lodge, wherein I could stay as long as I wish to. For under the sunshine, libraries are the best shelter spaces. If I could, I would move into the Piermont Morgan Library, the Freer Gallery of Art at the Smithsonian Institution, or the Vatican Library, where I would dwell in a tranquil and old-fashioned heaven, furnished with oriental carpets, mahogany armchairs, and French floor lamps. All physical comforts, sitting conveniences, and the serene aura are magnificent, but bibliothecae were "cases for books" and the essential soul of libraries is always their indispensable books, archives, and manuscripts, obscured or laureate pieces, that attract the special attention of my inquisitive spirits.

Perhaps, I should build at my home a tiny mini library, wherein I could stock up my personal collections and spend the prime time of my life. Talking to and touching them every day, I will then become the conscientious friend of these books; and vis-à-vis, they will be my loyal retinues, tendering to me their witty lines or enlightened pages any time at my request.

Now and then, I could look up to Nyaya and Descartes to search for their sagacious words when I am confused by the reality of the world. I may turn to *The Tale of Genji* to immerse myself in the ink of joys and tears of an ancient Japanese imperial family. I will flip open Marlowe's sonnets to apprehend the author's literary talents and to feel his amorous passion.

All fine books are the precious pieces of many authors. They normally embrace the experience, insights, and visions of these intellectuals or scholars. Many of these geniuses and genii have passed away and surrendered their pens for a long time. For their elaborations, some of them were tormented or sent to the guillotines, few acquired a fortune, and most hardly made their both ends meet.

Some of these thinkers and writers are still squatting by their busy, messy, and humble desks, continuously and consistently coining their words and uttering their statements, letter-by-letter and line-by-line. In spite of their time, in ancient eras or in the modern time; the origins they are akin to, Oriental or Caucasian, they all made contributions in forging theories, ideas, and concepts, that might be trivial or profound and known locally or universally.

Silkworms turn torpid only when they have bestowed all they are given. Like them, these noble men and women often devote unselfishly their entire lives to impart to others the fruits of their searches and researches. It is due to their dedication and their selflessness that thousands of books are originated; and millions of articles, composed. Innumerable readers, decade after decade, are thus inspired and motivated; and human societies, generation after generation, constantly moved forward.

Yesterday's history was once today's news and today's news will be yesterday's history. Bits and bytes, libraries acquire them all, inclusive of the tragedies of the Titanic sorrow and the Twin Towers' horror. While strolling towards a library miles away, I could hear the explosive bombardment of the Normandy thundering in the air and shaking its grounds. While hiding and pondering at a small carrel in a library, I could smell the scent of the fragrant Eden's roses that saturates the tall hall of the pyramid building and pervades its surroundings. In reality, they are from the massive volumes of books,

journals, and newspapers preserved in the library.

After a day indulging in the voluminous volumes of books, I would go home accompanied by Lao-Tse, Homer, and Szimborska. After many hours soaking in the library, I would stretch out on my bed, dreaming the virtuous "tao" of thousands of years ago, the invulnerable Hercules of the ancient epoch, the Poesie of the modern days, and the myths and fantasies of others, that would occupy my restless mind and soothe my poor soul. I then would not have any single nerve cell to summon to attend to the withering baby e-book and the chaotic jungle of the cyberworld.

●━━━━━━━━━━━━━━●

　　大學裡的圖書館，不但是校園的精神中心，是校園的主體建築；它是校園的靈魂，校園的無聲教授，默默地教誨啟發每一個進入圖書館的人；它是社區總體營造，推動終身學習的搖籃，更是國家民族文化延續與創造的泉源。接近它的人，可以跟古聖先哲作心靈的交會，可以跟當代名人談心，可以使人消除競逐名利之心，開拓胸襟懷抱，純任自然。使人上惘國難，下痛民窮。可以借千千萬萬人類心靈的眼睛，讓我們看到世界上最美好的事物；可以借成千上萬人類靈敏的耳朵，讓我們聽到世界上最悅耳的天籟之聲；可以借千千萬萬稟賦獨異的喉嚨，唱出人類心底的聲音，由此得到生命的舒暢，增加生命的深度與廣度，了解生命的意義與生活的目的。

圖書館正是為現在生活啟蒙⋯為文化精神長存不休，為未來勾勒文明遠景，安頓生命價值之所在⋯使人藏於斯，有其生命的安頓；休於斯，有其生命的閑適；習於斯，有其歷史的安頓；游於斯，有其文化的安頓。

圖書館是傳統文化的守護者，現在文化生活的指導者，未來生活文化的締造者，資訊流通的中樞。

圖書館像智慧的老子，佇立在校園當中，無為而無所不為，它從不拒絕於人，只有人拒絕於它⋯得意的人，進圖書館，會更得意；失意的人，進圖書館，不會再失意⋯在圖書館中，怒而讀之，躍然喜矣；憂而讀之，欣然樂矣；躁而讀之，悠然恬矣。

── 劉梅琴、王祥齡

DOES THE UNIVERSITY OF GUAM
LEAD THE CYBERWORLD?

Once upon a time, there was a Grand Academy of Lagado in a Pacific island. In the academy, there was a 20-foot square contrivance presented as follows:

The superficies was composed of
several bits of woods, about the bigness
of a die…. They were all linked
together by slender wires. These bits
of wood were covered on every square
with paper pasted on them, and on
these papers were written all their
language, in their several moods,
tenses, and declensions, but without
any order.

The machine was invented by a professor of the Academy, who employed it to turn vocabularies into frames with "the strictest computation of the general proportion … between the numbers of particles, nouns,

162

and verbs, and other parts of speech." The professor guided her / his young students, operated the engine six hours a day, and manufactured "several volumes in large folio...." By means of the invention,

the most ignorant person at a reasonable
charge, and a little bodily labour, may
write books in philosophy, poetry, law,
mathematics, and theology, without the
least assistance from genius or study.

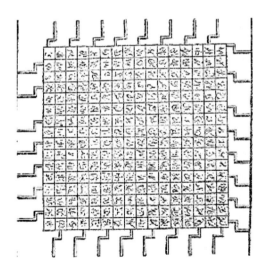

About three centuries later, T. H. Nelson conceived the first hypertext and created the Xanadu Project, which was aimed to digitise texts. In the meantime, science-fiction writers envisioned "mechanical educators," which could impress on human brains in a few minutes knowledge and skills, which would take a lifetime to acquire. Perhaps, both the hypertext and the imagined "educators" were inspired by the Lagadorian engine or even copied from the professor's invention at the Academy.

Later in the 1970s and the 1980s, high performance information networks and the Internet were developed. At the same time, T. Berners-Lee and his friends came up with the World Wide Web. And thus, we jumped from the industrial to the information age, a thrilling cyber world, wherein everyone is supposed to be able to reach out to the world for information instantly and transparently without the limit of time and space.

The Grand Academy was located in Lagado, the capital of Balnibari, as reported by J. Swift in his *Gulliver's Travels*. According to Swift, Balnibari was subject to the rule of the Flying or Floating Island monarch. And

Lagado was ninety leagues to the "north-east and by east" of the kingdom, that was about the distance of "four days and a half" travel.

I had a quick check on reference works including atlases and identified the Academy and Lagado, particularly in several literary books. I also retrieved citations of journal publications about the great institution. But so far, I have had no luck to locate information about Balnibari Island and the Flying kingdom, except the floating islands in Palau, in contemporary reference sources.

Since the Grand Academy of Lagado was located in a Pacific island and there are not very many great academies in the region even today, I would boldly assume that the Academy is the predecessor of the Territorial College of Guam. The former must have been discontinued sometimes in the 18th or 19th century because of the invasion of "modern civilization," the assault of supernatural forces, or the onslaught of formidable disasters. If the fantasies in the Swift's story could be traced in the real world, I would claim that because its forefathers invented the text-processing machine which

led to, about 300 years later, the Nelson's hypertext, the fundamental mechanism of the virtual reality, the University of Guam should be regarded as the earliest forerunner of today's cyber world.

Are you convinced with my assumption? Read the Swift's fascinating adventure, write up your hypotheses, do a search and research, collect relevant documents and evidences, and state your justification to substantiate or contest my assertion. This could be a challenging thesis. I will yield my copyright for this interesting research question. And the resourceful library professionals will assist you with the challenges of your research.

微 言 贅 語

Notes and Miscellanies

NOBODY'S FRIEND

My name is Gossip. I have no respect for justice.
I maim without killing, I break hearts and ruin lives,
I am cunning and malicious and gather strength with age.
The more I am quoted, the more I am believed.
My victims are helpless.
They cannot protect themselves against me
because I have no name and no face.
To track me down is impossible.
The harder you try, the more elusive I become.

I am nobody's friend.
Once I tarnish a reputation, it is never the same.
I topple governments and wreck marriages.
I ruin careers and cause sleepless nights,
heartaches, and indigestion.
I make innocent people cry in their pillows.
Even my name hisses. I am called GOSSIP.
I make headlines and headaches.

Before you repeat story, ask yourself:
Is it true? Is it harmless? Is it necessary?
If it isn't, don't repeat it.

為中國統一圖強而呼籲

　　英法革命，掀起一股民主潮流，世界各國相繼推翻君主政體。第二次世界大戰之後，由蘇聯共黨領導，歐、亞、非，包括中國的擴大領土，先後赤化。今天，波蘭、東德和東歐各國，先後揚棄共黨；蘇維埃聯邦解體，各共和國，包括俄羅斯，全部擺脫了共產主義。新的潮流在沖擊，共產制度即使苟延殘喘，亦將成為軀殼，如英日皇室，有名無實而已。

　　世局在變，在急劇的變。韓戰、越戰已經過去，柏林圍牆成了歷史；伊拉克侵佔柯威特，雖曾引起危機，受世界壓力，伊拉克不得不撤軍；巴爾幹各民族，以色列和巴勒斯坦之間，雖有紛爭，經聯合國、北約、和美國斡旋，亦在和平解決。

　　熱戰和冷戰已經過去，今天的世界面臨的是一場經濟大競賽。以前，日本帝國主義以優越的軍事力量，沒有征服世界。今天，日本卻在經濟競賽中，泰山壓頂，侵襲各大洲，買取世界。德國統一，歐盟成立，歐洲產生了新勢力，世界出現了新秩序。

　　當前，世局渾濁，東西不分，楚河漢界不復存在，舊的秩序打破了，世界勢力正在重新組合。展望未來，美俄再度聯盟，歐美日互相抗衡，或歐美對峙，孰可料，何不可料？

　　際此變局，正是中國求取民主自由，統一圖強的好時機。蓋蘇聯解體之後，各共和國自求發展，中國因此可以無後顧之憂，得以暫時喘息。而且當此世界秩序重新整合之際，中國正可化敵為友，與世界列強，和平相處。國際形勢大好，中國是分是合，為弱為強，今天是關鍵時機。

　　兩次大戰，中國都有轉弱圖強的機會，不幸都沒有善於把握，聽任失去。第一次大戰，德俄酣戰於歐，中國則陷於軍閥混戰，民命交疲，無從任何建設。第二次大戰，中國犧牲千百萬軍民，損失無數財產，最後戰勝日本。戰後，日本從廢墟中建立起來，四、五十年功夫，一變成為首富強國。中國不但沒有保持勝利果實，反而窮於內外戰爭，文鬥武鬥，兄弟鬩牆，自相殘殺；時至今日，仍然政治分裂，經濟遠落於日本和列強之後。

　　世界在變，中國也在變。前代英豪，一一逝去，舊時思想包袱，政治恩怨，早應劃下句點，謀求解決。況且中國大陸和臺灣，唇齒相依，傳統和地緣，同屬一體；兩地人民，都是黃炎子孫，骨肉同胞。無論從何說起，雙方沒有鋪不平的鴻溝。此時此際，論情論理，中國若不能溝通內部，和平統一，進而建設圖強；而今而後，中華民族，永遠休矣！

　　近年，臺灣已放棄與大陸對立的政策。經過四十餘年的努力，今天的台灣，經濟上已經建立相當規模，政治上大步邁向民主自由，提倡人權。臺灣既已打開門戶，中國大陸的領導，亦應視民族千年萬世的利益，中華後代億萬子孫的福祉，高於黨的原則，重於私人的得失，放棄霸權心態，摒除武力恫嚇，敞開胸懷，坦誠歡迎臺灣的提議，積極回應，立即坐下商談，互為折衝，互為忍讓。中國若能因此溝通，進而和平統一，以大陸龐大人力，豐富資源，結合臺灣相當成功之經驗，全力投注於政治改革和經濟建設，一、二十年之後，中國當可與美日和歐洲並駕齊驅，成為富強之國；中華人民，亦將享有民主自由和富足的生活。果爾如此，中華民族幸甚，中國和普天下的中國人幸甚！

德國統一四年的經驗

德國駐菲副大使施博德CHRISTIAN SEEBODE近訪關島，曾至德國友誼社，發表演說，原講稿長約萬字。值茲臺海兩岸各舉國統綱領、江八點，尋求統一途徑之際，特依原稿內容，摘寫要點，提供兩岸同胞及領導階層參考。

德國統一以前，背有許多歷史包袱，影響統一。在歐陸，德國地大人眾，經濟強大，歐洲各國不能全無考慮，接納一個強大統一的德國。大西洋兩岸均有疑懼，恐怕統一的德國，重提日耳曼帝國時的地緣說；民族主義重新抬頭；人民再次結成暴力，威脅鄰邦。萊茵河彼岸，一直不願見到「條頓大帝國」；奧地利雖有意「中歐」政體，歷史教訓在先，亦恐再受德國的控制。大西洋彼岸，不無擔心「天下萬國，德意志為上」的意念，借屍還魂。而且統一的德國，處理與西方盟國、俄羅斯，以及近鄰各國的關係，問題尤其錯綜複雜。所幸德國統一之後，一切疑懼煙消雲散。統一的德國，參加了北約和歐盟，反而促進勢力平衡，保持歐洲的穩定。而且統一的德國，已成了主導力量，促使歐洲單一市場的實現；規劃政策，引導北歐、中東歐各國，將來適時參與歐盟。

　　德國統一，牽涉政治、經濟，及貨幣制度的改變，公共建設、裁軍和外資等問題。統一後，政治上首須解決東德的黨政幹部。甄選和留用眾多的地方幹部，困難重重。統一東西德不同的法制和法律，同為棘手的問題。另外，選舉各級民意代表，產生地方和聯邦政府區劃地方行政權責，更屬艱困。經四年變革，東德終於擺脫共黨獨裁，變為民主社會，欣欣向榮，受到國際注目。

　　在經濟上，東德的人民企業，原本落後，冗員累累，產品不能與外界競爭。農業佔地過大，生產超過市場需要。自由市場興起之後，產業和土地的所有權，過剩的勞工，均不易處理。一個信託機構，應運而生；於一九九四年之前，將所有人民企業，全部化為私有。統一後，東德的經濟曾一時衰退，因西德和外來的投資，很快復甦起飛。

　　因有國際承諾，德國統一後，不得不大量裁減軍員軍備。結果是，國家人民軍隊除了少數下級官兵外，全部裁撤。撤軍過程中，重要的措施計有：徵收新兵時，東西德互至對方地區徵取；西德將軍官學校及其他重要軍事機構，遷移至東德地區；軍中官兵，輪調服務，以增加認識全國的領土和同胞。

　　統一前，東西德各為蘇聯集團和東歐的主要貿易國。統一後，因幣值、工資和產品價格高昇，進口需求減少，使得東德與中東歐的貿易，幾乎化為烏有。但西德與該地區的貿易，卻相對急速增加，因此以全國總貿易量計，統一的德國，又成了中東歐各國的首要貿易國家。

東歐各國對蘇聯集團強迫貿易，記憶猶新，並曾竭力掙扎，設法擺脫俄國影響。德國捲土重來，擁有強大的經濟力量，各國亦頗擔心，恐懼再度失去獨立，因此與德國擴大經濟關係，均有爭議。德國內部，亦有正反意見。惟德國統一，於今四年，事實證明，與德國擴大經貿，相關各國，均有利無弊。

沒有人是孤島，每個人都是大陸的一小塊，任何人的死亡，都會使我減少，因為我與人類有著切身的關係。

—— Jone Donne

德國統一及其與東鄰關係

原作者： Christian Seebode

　　本文為德國駐菲律賓副大使施博德在關島德國友好聯誼社，以英文所發表之講稿，《關島太平洋日報》有專文報導。本文根據原講稿摘譯，經施博德副大使許可。正如原文引言所說，德國雖遠隔重洋，其統一過程，和政治、經貿之變革發展，對於亞太地區，有著重大關係。臺海兩岸，距離雖遠，同為華夏疆土，目標終應統一。東西德統一之過程和經驗，可為中國統一之重要借鏡。文中所述，德國統一前後，對外之地理環境、歷史背景、國際疑慮；對內之政治、經濟、法律、行政、貨幣制度之變革統一，財產所有權之處理，裁減兵員、地方交通、電信建設、投資，以及對外貿易發展，各項細節，尤值兩岸同胞和領導人物，準備未來商談統一參考。

一、統一背景

　　今日世界事務，牽一髮而動全局。東西德統一四年，其國家變動，對於世局，亦有重大影響。茲就德國統一之重大環節，及其對政治、經濟，及公共生活各方面之影響，略述管見，就教於方家。論述當中，特別著重下列四項問題：（一）政治突變，（二）統一過程之艱困，（三）德國八千萬人民之經濟負擔，以及（四）東德與其鄰邦之關係，包括與前共產經濟体關係之變遷。

　　茲先介紹德國一九九〇年前後之政治和經濟歷史。大戰之後，德國被分割成東西兩部分，東德據有三分之一的領土，陷入蘇聯和波蘭勢力。一九四六年，鐵幕下垂，使德國變成政治、思想、和經濟不同的兩個政体：德意志聯邦共和國和德意志民主共和國；東西方列強對峙，東西德也成了雙方的有力前鋒；冷戰僵持，核子戰爭的毀滅性，脅逼人心。西德幸為西歐共同體一員，創造經濟奇績，分享其經濟成長及利益；東德淪為蘇聯附庸，行動受制，不幸墮落。依據共產經濟体之水準，其經濟雖頗有成，但與西德經濟相比，顯見缺失重重；當西德激起第三次經濟革命，即電子微導体之革命後，東德之經濟發展，尤其相形見拙。東德雖竭盡努力，希冀趕上西德，但一切努力，皆徒勞無功。當其政權以極大之財政及政治代價，仍難以維持人民生活水準；當電子時代擴散至各邊遠的鄉村之後，東德制度的破綻，開始暴露了出來。人民怨聲載道，不滿國家的經濟發展，反抗人權被剝奪；要求自由，過較好的生活，旅行不受限制；要於勞動之餘，分享工作成果。於是人民共起揚棄共產獨裁，不服共產政權，終而導致了東德政權的崩潰；其蘇聯盟邦，亦隨後瓦解。一九八九年十一月，柏林圍牆拆毀，新的時代從此開始，一年之後，東西德統一。

二、政治環境

　　德國人民對於統一的夢，都以為成了空想，德意志不過是一個地緣學上的名詞而已。曾經分裂、曾經敵對而立的東西德，現在卻必須面對事實，應付歷史包袱，即歐洲大陸能否容納一個統一的、八千萬眾多人口的德國；德國在歐洲共同体和北大西洋公約中，雖尚能平安無事，其地理面積畢竟太大，其經濟勢力畢竟太強。東歐風吹草動，局勢未可預測，歐洲大陸出現一個強大的德國，能否風平浪靜？大西洋兩岸均有疑慮，擔心統一的德國，會否重拾舊夢，再提日耳曼帝國時代的地緣之說？民族主義會否再次抬頭？人民會否再次結合成為一股強大的暴力，威脅鄰邦？值得注意的是，除俄國之外，德國陸連的鄰國最多，包括丹、荷、比、盧、法、瑞、奧、捷、波等九國。德國的統一，無疑將影響其與陸連各鄰國的關係。同時值得注意的是，二次大戰之後，萊茵河彼岸，一直不放心波羅的海與阿爾比斯山之間的「條頓大帝國」。
霍布斯堡曾經鼓吹，以多腦皇朝時代諸國為基礎，建
立「中歐洲」；奧地利雖頗重視此理想，但有歷史教
訓，始終恐受德國的控制。最後，捷克與波蘭，對於
德國的統一，是否亦有敏感？

　　廣而言之，往昔「白日之下，德意志為上。」
借屍還魂之疑慮，是否不利於德國與大西洋彼岸的
關係？冷戰時期，德國受盟邦支持，曾在自由世界，
扮演重要地位，維持柏林為自由城市；統一的德國，
將何以盡其對昔日盟國的義務？世界秩序重組之後，
德國亦須面對俄國問題。二十世紀雖經二次大戰，
德俄兩國及其人民，始終暗通款曲，有著藕斷絲連的
關係。戰時的對立，以及冷戰的磨擦，并未減輕兩國
人民互相尊重，對彼此文化的重視。即使國際局勢處
於極度緊張，兩國亦能維持並加強彼此之經濟關係，
因之而成了歐洲大陸的穩定力量。捷克和波蘭鄰邦，
因有歷史前例，卻無法苟同德國的作為，俄德重新諒
解，他們是否會成了犧牲品？

　　以上憂慮，今時過境遷，一切均未成為事實。
德國第一次全國普選之後，聯邦總理柯爾對國會的
演說中，曾經強調，統一的德國，將加倍努力，盡
其兄弟之邦的義務，繼續促進歐洲共同體。全德加盟

於北大西洋公約組織，以及歐洲聯盟兩項事實，將促進歐洲勢力平衡，保持穩定。自此之後，事實上德國已經成了主導力量，促使歐洲單一市場的實現，并同時規劃政策，以便斯堪的那各國和奧地利加入歐洲聯盟。兩週以前，德國剛卸下歐洲聯盟主席的職位；事實證明，德國主持歐盟時，已盡努力，使中歐及東歐各國，傾向於歐洲聯盟，以遂爾後各自適時加盟的目的。

三、東德方面的改變

以上所述，為德國統一的背景，現且談談德國統一與東鄰的關係，特別是有關傳統的經濟關係，以及統一過程中，從社會主義經濟，過度到自由市場經濟的轉變。柏林重新統一，問題繁多，當另作討論；本文所述，著重於新聯邦（東德）各省的諸種問題。

德國統一，史無前例，從傳統和因統一而產生的轉變觀看，尤顯得其過程，錯綜特殊。德國歷史，從未經歷兩個不同的政治制度，結合為一；兩個不同的經濟制度，合而為一；兩種貨幣制度，成為統一的幣制；東德落後的地方設施，得以建設提高，使得人民大眾，分享現代的生活水準；而且，東德擁有華沙公約國內，僅次於蘇聯的強大軍隊，公約解散之後，其軍隊必須裁減復員。茲將諸多問題列述於下：

（一）政冶制度

　　自由民主的社會中，從來沒有一個政治制度，自行宣告解體，也沒有以「工人階級」統治的共產黨，及其群眾組織、或公安機構，自行宣告解散。這些組織實際上與地方行政機構密切關連，以個人而言，每人所負政治或地方行政責任，實難以區分。東德佔有全國三分之一的領土，困難的問題在於處理原先統治這部分領土的東德共黨基層幹部。解散、留用，如何甄選？而且管理現代民主國家的行政工作，除技術和知識之外，還有其他要求，因而使得處理共黨幹部的問題，更形困難。另外，舊日德意志聯邦共和國的全部法制，必須放棄，而採用「第二德國」的法律；同時，以前因思想相異而產生的法律，亦不能不予顧慮，斷然放棄不用。東德共黨於四十年代後期，廢棄了地方行政區劃，德國統一之後，又恢復了縣市行政範圍，地方和新聯邦政府，亦由選舉產生新的民意代表。與此同時，各級政府民主權責，也逐次劃分并建立起來。基於東西德雙方，人力均屬有限，統一之後，建立三權分立的民主制度，困難不難想像，但四年之後，經驗證明，這些努力，并未枉費。德國統一，史無前例，其經過多為一邊摸索，一邊進行，錯失難免。惟大體而言，把東德共黨獨裁政體，脫胎換骨，轉變成為民主、興興向榮、并受國際刮目相看的社會，全部過程，堪稱十分成功。總之，今日的東德，已無人響往昔日的制度了。

（二）經濟制度

在東歐集團之內，以前東德的經濟制度，原來甚受重視，認為是最好的，俄、波、羅、保等各國人民，都十分響往東德的財富。西方前往訪問的政商人士，亦有同感，認為東德的經濟制度，雖有瑕疵，生產工具落後，但一切尚算不差。柏林圍牆，隔夜倒下後，令人驚詫，東德受共黨控制的經濟制度，一旦公諸於世，其殘缺不全，令人難以置信，西方政商人士的信心，也立即化為烏有。

東德經濟情況，原來如此：人民所有的企業，冗員累累；生產機構，已非廠礦，而成了工業博物館；工業生產，全然應因共產經濟体的需求，毫未考慮國內的供求關係；貨品價格，非以實際價值訂定，因而無法與西方企業產品競爭；蘇維埃式的農業，佔地面積太大，致使廣大美好的國家土地，變成了農業荒漠；農業生產，遠超市場的需求，農業勞動力過剩，又無法轉業於其他行業。

尤甚者，隨著自由市場經濟興起之後，所謂「人民所有」的制度，必須廢棄。然而，各種產業的所

181

有權，現又誰屬？空中樓閣的工人階級、當時的佔用者、抑或以前的所有權人？所有權狀如何認定？以前的私有土地，建有道路、房屋和公共設施；許多老舊工廠，產品滯銷，卻擁有過多的優秀勞動力；解決此等問題，削足就履，艱困多多。因此，一個特別信託機構，應運而生，將所有「人民企業」，於一九九四年以前，全部私有化。在新環境下，許多「舊工業中心」雖已不能存在，但舊時的創意和精神，仍有可用之處。是時，極其重要者，為來自西德和國外的投資。據統計，新聯邦各省的投資總額，於一九九三年為一千四百億（140b）馬克，一九九四年增加到了一千六百億（160b）馬克，其中三分之二，係來時舊聯邦（西德）各省；其餘三分之一，大部分來自歐洲聯盟各國，但亦有少部分來自美國和東歐國家者。統一之後，東德方面的國家生產毛額，於一九九一年減低了三分之一，爾後又逐年提高，其增加率為一九九二年百分之八，一九九三年百分之六，一九九四年百分之十。凡此足以顯示，東德的經濟，終又起死回生，重新起飛。惟因歐洲普遍失業的棘手問題，仍限東德於困境之中。一如西德，東德現在的失業率為百分之八至百分之十之間。

（三）貨幣制度

東德的經濟制度，由共黨控制，過度到市場經濟，務必有統一的貨幣配合。具體而言，即以西德馬克，根據合理的兌換率，將東德馬克取而代之。一九四九年，德意志聯邦共和國創始之初，曾有變換貨幣的經驗。然而前車之鑑，並不足減少此次貨幣變換，所可能產生的危機，因為在變換過程中，一方面必須有足夠的錢幣，供應東德一千六百萬人民之需；另一方面，政府和聯邦銀行必須考慮，控制通貨澎脹；許多個人的不公和損失，固且不談。一九九〇年六月，西德錢幣開始輸往東德，七月一日，東德數百萬人民，有了新印的西德馬克，用以取代解體了的德意志民主共和國的舊貨幣。許多在西德有親友的人，也因此發了一些財。四年之後，回顧檢討，此次統一貨幣，有利有弊。經濟制度有了變革，貨幣理當統一，但因政治因素，兌換率未免訂得過高，因而增加了貨幣發行量，進而加強了人民的購買力。正當此時，德國的經濟又處於惡性循環的低潮，終而加速了通貨澎脹，同時，過度發行貨幣，對於利率亦有深遠的影響，時至今日，仍遺有不良後果。

（四）公共設施

綜上所述，可見東德政治、經濟和貨幣制度變革過程，需用龐大無比的經費，此為德國納稅人，對其國家統一，所肩負的財政重擔。尤甚者，德國每年還須調度為數千億（100b）美元，投資新聯邦各省，而且未來十年，仍須繼續該項鉅額投資。今日的東德，無論城市或鄉村，處處都在建設，欣欣向榮。在政府鼓吹「東向」政策之下，以前坑凹不平的道路，已經全部修復；戰前建造的橋樑，已予翻修加強，以應三千年代的交通需求。數千公里的鐵道，也予以重新舖設和聯接；昔日破舊的叮噹火車，現已不復再見。前因國家分裂，造成交通系統紛亂，為了克服其中困難，全國的交通流向和系統，已予重新規劃，作了九十度的調整，使原來南北向的交通系統，轉變為東西向。以前，東德為了社會主義的生產，完全不顧環境保護；今天，環保已經成了政治和經濟活動的主要環節。各地建立了污水處理廠，煙囪加上了過濾器，垃圾有妥善處理。新的車輛，無煙塵催化器，不予註冊登記，強制執行。最大的變化，則是德國電信公司，於不到四年之內，不聲不響，將東德方面殘舊不全，仍以戰前機械操作的電信網路，全部予以更新，提升到現代水準，使用電子設備和纖維電纜。以前，東德人民申請電話，必須等待十五年以上，現在的德國電信公司，一週之內，包供電話使用。

　　東德各方面的發展，費用浩大，但用其所當，並不可惜。蓋東德一千六百萬同胞，飽經滄桑，歷盡威瑪共和、納粹獨裁、冷戰、俄國佔領、以及共黨統治之後，應有較好的現在和將來。因此之故，新聯邦各省獲得了鉅大的國家和私人投資，數額之鉅，世界任何地區的投資，無可望其項背；於是，東德終於成了全歐最為發達的地區。

（五）裁減兵員

　　在德國統一過程中，不能不談裁軍和安全問題。除蘇聯之外，東德原來擁有前共黨集團國家中，最為強大的軍隊。柏林圍牆拆除之後，隔夜之間，這支強大無比的軍隊，成為新民主德國的一部分。當時，德國為歐洲安全合作會議裁軍條約的簽字國，承諾裁軍，必須將西德三軍，減少現員。統一之後，國家又增加了一支政治和軍事均無必要的宮庭皇軍，數量遠超德國對國際裁軍承諾的許可。此外，德國又必須處理八千七百個武器系統，以及三千五萬頓庫存彈藥。總而言之，德國的裁軍數量，其比率之大，僅次於俄國而已。國家人民軍的兵員，除了極少數的將級以下官兵之外，得予全部裁撤復員。統一過程中，西德的三軍部隊，對於軍隊的調配統一，建樹甚豐。其措施為：東西德互在對方地區，徵收新兵員；將軍官學校及其他重要軍事機構，遷往東德地區；軍中官兵，輪調服務，使更為瞭解祖國的另外一部分地區及同胞。

四、國際貿易

德國統一之前，西德為西方在東歐的首要貿易國；同時，東德又為前共產經濟体中，除蘇聯之外的第二大貿易國。因之，德國統一之後，對於東歐的全般貿易往還，自然會有舉足輕重的地位。二次大戰之後，蘇聯集團的擴張，曾影響了東歐各國的經貿，使其脫離與西歐的關係；當時，共產經濟体中的貿易，係受政治需要，而非經濟因素的支配。德國統一之後，貿易不再受政治牽制，被迫而為；為了更好的利益，以及地理鄰近的緣故，並在所謂「回歸歐洲」的前題之下，統一的德國，重新成為中歐和東歐貿易主体的事實，自然無足置疑。

與西德統一之後，東德的貨幣兌換率和工資，突飛猛漲；東德廠商的產品價格，亦隨著提高，因而失去了中歐和東歐的市場。一九九三年，東德輸往中東歐的出口額，減到了一九九〇年的百分之廿以下。同時，因為東德不再需要當地和中東歐的產品，其從中東歐的進口，亦大量減少。因此，德國統一的結果，幾乎使得東德與中東歐地區的進出口貿易，一掃而空。一般希望，隨著跟進的西德與中東歐的貿易，將彌補東德失去的貿易量。驚異的是，今天希望終於成了事實，西德與中東歐的貿易，果然增長迅速，很快超越了東德以前失去的數量。於是，德國現在仍然是中東歐地區進口和出口的首要貿易國家。首先，中東歐輸往德國的出口，開始大幅增長。其中，波蘭於一九九三年的輸出為二十三億（2.3b）美元，其數量恰好等於其官方報導的國家赤字。值茲德國經濟衰退，全部外貿減少之際，其與中東歐的貿易，反而急速增長，此種發展，意義非常。循此發展趨勢，假定中東歐仍能繼續供應德國的需要，且對其進口市場，不加限制，德國目前的經濟復甦，極有可能擴大德國與中東歐地區的貿易，並加快其增長的速度。

德國統一所需的財務，大部分依賴資本市場支持，因此，對於銀行利率，有其重大影響，於是引起了中東歐地區的擔心，深恐因此而提高資金成本，延緩各國的經濟改革。事實上，利率雖曾提高，但為時未久，因受世界性經濟衰退的影響，長期利率，反而減到了幾近有史以來的最低限度。

蘇聯集團的強制貿易，迫使東歐各國，蒙受損失，記憶猶新，令人遺憾。然而，德國捲土重來，其強大的經濟力量，會否影響各國獨立，亦屬令人憂懼。以東歐而言，各國均在竭力掙扎，設法擺脫俄羅斯的強大地緣引力；對於德國統一之後，其巨大無比的壓力，亦難衷心歡迎。因此之故，東歐各國，對於擴大與德國的經濟關係，曾有極為複雜的爭議；而在德國方面，亦有正反兩面的意見。然而與德國擴大經濟關係，相關各國，均蒙其利。德國統一，於今四年，現在事實証明，與德國擴大經濟關係，已非問題，當今惟一的問題，僅是「如何」擴大與德國的經濟關係，最為有利。

在群眾中，你生活在當時的時代；在孤獨中，你生活在所有的時代。一個人的心靈，如果思想寧靜，心境和諧，便是世界上最幽靜的地方。

—— 啟麥

核能發電與科技應用

核能發電，猶如其他科技發明的應用，爭議甚多，公說公理，婆說婆理。

鐵路引進中國，曾遭受反對

十八、九世紀交替時，工業開始發展，生產逐漸增加，為了輸送產品，馬匹成了重要的運輸工具，但也引起反彈。有人說：馬匹成群，行人如何走路；到處馬糞，臭氣薰天，不但有礙觀瞻，也污染空氣。保護動物的人，提出抗議，反對利用牲畜，苛待動物；反對駕馬長途飛奔，負荷載重。

十九世紀末，鐵路引進中國，士大夫群起反對，認為火車頭會撞死行人、耕牛，破壞鄉土風水，而拆毀了初建的路段，延遲了中國鐵路建設。

今日，資訊時代來臨，電腦科技發達，肉身與機器混合人體，已見怪不怪。機器人猶在發展，頗有取人類而代之的氣勢。恐龍和人類的許多先祖，都已一一絕種，科學技術不斷發展，人類難免也有滅種的可能。許多先進先賢，已開始恐懼，懷疑科技生化研究，是否應無窮無盡，終至危害人類自身的生存？

文明帶來便利舒適及副作用

　　宇宙不斷演變，人們的腦子愈來愈發達，花樣愈
來愈多，創造發明，日新月異。然而天下事物，有正
便有負；每樣創新發明，固然帶給人們便利、舒適、
或享受，也產生連帶副作用。

　　先祖鑽木取火，人類得以熟食、取暖，更有了
無限的能源，但火也引來了大災大亂，有史以來，
為火燒死燒傷的人，何止千千萬？科學家鑽研物性物
理，利用原子、電子和化學分子，創造了許多新鮮事
物，提供人們使用，助長人類文明。不幸的是，原子
彈、生化武器、細菌等等，也被用於戰爭，荼毒殺害
人類。雖然如此，人們前進了一步，少有倒退不前的
事。人類擺脫了猿猴，站了起來，雙腳行走，固然有
絆腳、跌撞的危險，但始終沒有再用四肢爬行。先祖
發現熟食，我們就不怕火燒水燙，不再茹毛飲血了。

車諾比事件未影響核電發展

　　汽車肇禍，飛機失事，時時都有，令人驚心。
一九九七年，全世界飛機失事死亡九百三十人，全
美汽車意外，奪去四萬二千四百人的生命。然而每逢
旅行旺季，機票仍是一位難求；上下班尖鋒時刻，高
速公路仍舊塞車，人們處變不驚，照樣坐飛機、開汽

車，好像死亡都是他人的事。

核電有紐約三哩島和烏克蘭車諾比驚動世人的意外，但一九九〇年，全世界的應用核能反應爐，仍有三百六十八個單元；到了一九九八年，且增加到了四百三十六個單元。

時代加速演變；機器人、醫學生物、基因科學，迅速發展。展望前程，人類沒有被取代、亡族滅種以前，勢必會繼續不斷鑽研，推向機靈世界，創造科學怪人。

世界由渾沌，轉變為農牧、工商、以至於今日的E世代，創造發明頻頻，許多人認為是文明的進步。各種新的發明，有污染，有溫室效應，破壞生態，甚至把人類推向滅亡的邊緣，許多人認為是文明的倒退。

維持世外桃源，就無經濟奇績

四、五十年以前，臺灣高山長青，綠水長流，不失為美麗島。今日寶島南北，高樓大廈，鱗次櫛比，煙突處處，工商業欣欣向榮；公路交錯，機車汽車，擁塞一團。有人思古懷舊，想念臺北雲高天青，鳥語花香。但若臺灣一直保留處女地，維持世外桃源，依靠無煙囪工業，依靠日月潭排水發電，大概就沒有臺北市的世貿大廈，沒有經濟奇績；也不會成為亞洲的四小龍，大陸同胞捨命偷渡的地方了。

　　小和尚初下凡界，看到師父所稱的女人虎，憑心憑性，愈看愈可愛。上帝創造伊甸園，神斧神工，盡善盡美，夏娃、亞當，還是偷吃了禁果。不然，世界只有夏娃和亞當，上帝創造萬物，何以為用？衡情度理，偷吃禁果，或許還是天意神差。世祖失樂園以後，人類念念不忘樂園，盼望那裡的小橋、流水、山林、草木；卻又世世代代，流血流汗，不斷嘗試金石利器、鐵船飛甲、太空梭、核能、和機器人。火有致命之險，飛蛾見火，卻奮不顧身，撲向前去；河豚有毒，人們貪食，敢冒大險。庸碌、貪婪、軟弱、矛盾，這些就是人性、人類的大千世界。

水果愈撿愈少，是非愈撿愈多。
學講話，要六年；學不講話，要六十年。
　　　　　　　　　　　　　——民間諺語

李前總統登輝先生憂心愁煩了

　　李前總統登輝先生於二〇〇〇年總統大選，政權移轉，失去國家元首的權位，被迫離開國民黨主席的位置以後，言語行動，激烈反常，掉轉槍頭，衝擊培植扶養他成長茁壯，進而飛黃騰達的母親黨。著書立說，懷恨國民黨，指國民黨為外來政權。稍後，立法委員選舉時，他拉下往昔面具，明目張膽，與臺獨聯手，力挺異黨，抨擊往日與他胼手胝足，共同為臺灣地區人民，為中華民國，為中國國民黨，流血流汗，一起打拼的同志手足，親自指定的接班人馬，指控他們背離了他的路線。接著，北高市長選舉，他一面高分貝地批扁治國無能，又與扁併肩站臺，力挺民進黨，反反覆覆，神志頗似錯亂糊塗。

　　第一次政黨輪替以後，為時不久，李前總統的言語行動，一百八十度大轉彎；忘恩負義，與親密同志，反目成仇。李先生到處奔走，大聲疾呼，說他愛臺灣，拼民主。與扁關係，若即若離，態度失常。有人指出，李失去權位，也失去了政治舞臺，不耐孤單，不堪寂寞。有人反思，或許國人欠缺政治包容，虧欠了李先生，沒有給他高度頌揚，沒有給他調適的空間。心理學家分析，李的行為是一種戀母情結，逆

193

倫弒父人格的表現。這些說辭和分析，都言之成理。
其實，李前總統的言行急轉彎，態度反覆失常，有單
純的因素，也有複雜的時空背景。

　　回顧歷史，在帝皇專制時代，世界各國，改朝
換代，必有激烈傾軋，流血戰爭，被推翻的皇帝和
皇室，不是被流放，被監禁，就是被荼毒，被殺害，
其情其景，慘絕人環。中國歷朝歷代，政權交替，
末代君皇，誰能全身，誰能逃過劫亂？宋末，元騎兇
悍，四面追逼，帝兵逃循不了，終於投身粵海而盡。
清亡，溥儀有幸，保住一命，但一生為人傀儡，聽任
擺佈，其羞辱，其痛苦，也是悔莫出生帝皇家了。

　　專制皇帝，交出了皇位，也交出了腦袋。世界
政治民主以後，政權移轉，避免了流血，也減少了犧
牲。但許多初行民主政治的國家，制度不夠成熟，政
權交替時，卸任的元首或政治人物，仍是難以全身而
退，逃脫不了災難。近二十多年以來，許多亞洲國家
的總統或政要，交了權位以後，都出了問題。

　　菲律賓的馬可士，選舉失敗，離開權位後，訴訟
接踵而來，最後懷恨終老異鄉；身後訟案未了，其夫
人的鞋履，也是人們茶餘飯後的談笑資料。其後的伊
斯特拉大，被迫下臺，立即陷於貪瀆的訴訟之中。南
韓的大統領朴正熙和盧泰愚，與黑金掛勾，交卸了政

權，噹啷進了監獄。馬來西亞的副總理安華，因為黨派鬥爭，身繫囹圄，有理洗不清。印尼的蘇哈托，交出總統大位以後，飽受訴訟驚惶，終日不得安寧。

歷史事實，如影隨形，李前總統看在眼裡、驚在心頭。二〇〇〇年總統大選，國民黨失敗後，中央黨部前面群情激動，憤怒抗議，矛頭對準黨主席。李先生心知肚明，看到了菲、韓、印、馬等國歷史的端倪，也意識到以前下台君皇的悲哀。再者，總統選舉期間，李玩手段，大搞興票案，耍陰謀，暗通綠營，打擊連宋，傷天害理，人心難平。有朝一日，政黨二次輪替，拉法葉等軍購弊案，一定會擴大升高，牽涉國家最高層面。日轉月移，藍軍歸來，鴻禧山莊、新瑞都開發案，其中黑手，恐怕都會一一被揪了出來。

歲月飛逝，二〇〇四年又是總統選舉了。李前總統又不斷放話，說連戰發瘋了，要想當總統；連宋當選，他要流亡國外，他的頭殼要被砍了。這些當然是有目的、刺激性的反助選語言，但也真實反映了李內心的驚懼恐慌。

李前總統曾受日本教育，充當皇軍。臺灣光復之初，國府官員失當，執行中央政策有了偏差，因而引起臺灣同胞的失望和不滿。李前總統於末任數年，竭力要走向世界舞台，建立政治聲望，但受中共嚴重打壓，寸步難行，出不了場面，也損害了尊嚴。凡此種種，有形無形，都影響了李先生的人格形成，因而其心底深處，對於中國的認同，自有異樣的伊底牢結。不過他形諸文字，痛恨國民黨，無情無義，以實際行動，打擊同志，以心理學簡單的刺激和反應原理來分析，或許則是被迫辭去黨主席，受到群眾憤怒抗議，心中惱恨，直接反射的行為。

李前總統利用國民黨，常年執政，集黨政軍權於一身，形成帝皇心態，享受君皇權力，走了馬可士、朴正熙等的歪路，與黑金掛勾，難保清白。為了權位，一時合縱，一時連橫，先後鬥倒了林、郝，凍結了宋楚瑜，明槍暗箭，破壞連戰。今天，他沒有了權位，眾叛親離，心中自忖，真是烽火連天，四面楚歌。因此之故，他要另起念頭，憑著往昔的魔力，拼了八十多歲的老命，組織臺聯黨，明明白白，搞起了臺獨，實實在在，投靠綠營去了。李先生顛顛倒倒，反覆無常，內心自然錯綜複雜。不過其失去權位以後的所作所為，簡單看起來，也只是他憂心忡忡，驚恐懼怕之餘，為他自己的身體安全和歷史聲譽，尋求一個擋風躲雨的保護傘罷了。

●────────────────────────●

饅頭大不過蒸籠格，死人硬不過棺材板。

A GENTLEMAN VS A CROOK

In today's diverse, democratic, and complex society, it is not easy to distinguish the principle of the right and the wrong. Each individual has different interpretation and attitude toward any social events. Everyone can make a strong argument in support of his points of view according to his value system and belief.

The religious fanatics can empower hundreds of men and women gathering to take their own lives. The malicious politicians have the superpower of persuading people to do whatever to satisfy their ego and greed. They

197

can lead the mob to wage wars against, and massacre millions of, their follow human beings. The vagueness between the right and the wrong and between a gentleman and a cunning crook is surely the source of trouble of today's chaotic and irresponsible world.

The *Book of I* 易經, a Chinese classic, devotes a major portion to distinguishing the attributes of a gentleman from those of a crook. Generations after generations, many scholars also have devoted various discussions on the different behaviors of a great man from those of a wicked person. From these philosophic illustrations, one may learn some basic, timeless, and still valid principles that define what is right, what is wrong, who is a gentleman, and who is a crook.

In the modern democratic world, when officials or representatives are elected, the principles may offer suggestions to those candidates on how to behave themselves in seeking support of the public. The distinction of these personal traits of a gentleman from those of a crook may give guides to the masses to whom they should cast their votes. The different traits also can be held as a yardstick to appraise the direction of oneself and other people in society. Be advised that God created all men, but they fall to the evil temptations. No one is perfect; one can only be more or less of a gentleman or a crook. For equality, a man always can be substituted with a woman in the article.

A great man always has a will to serve his community, country, or the world. He always lives for and thinks of others. Whatever he does will not aim to gain for himself. He will speak straight forward; will not try to please other people; and, very often, may not succeed in achieving his goals. A cunning crook works for and thinks of only himself. He will talk sweetly, act gently, and try all his means to please others. Quite often, a crook will win support in the community because of his sweet tongue.

A great man often has insight views toward various events of the world, which may not be accorded with the general belief held by the community. His ideas will often collide with the common expectations of the public. He may then become alienated, unpopular, and even become the target of criticism in the community.

An evil person, on the contrary, will try his best to learn the appetite of people. He does not have the moral

principle of the right and the wrong and will not appraise the reality of the real world. He will say whatever the masses want and try to please their appetite. Often, the popularity of such a selfish person will be skyrocketed high in the community, and most time he will reap what he has contrived in his mind.

A gentleman will win support from the public on the basis of his competencies, credentials, and confidence he has established in the past. He will not attempt to defeat his competitors by means of undermining others. On the other hand, a crook will use all possible means, including dirty tricks, defamation, and sabotage, to beat his opponents. He will not take account of any costs for winning a contest.

Because a gentleman is candid, sincere, and honest, a crook will know his intentions and courses of actions very well; while a crook is always disguising, shrewd, and canny, no one knows what really is in his mind. A gentleman usually holds his beliefs and will not compromise with a crook; who, on the contrary, will bow to the former pretentiously when he needs to. The different personal qualities often make the former hard to agree upon by others, and enable the latter to gain approval from the public.

A gentleman will often try to accept a crook and forgive his evil behaviors. He always hopes the crook will sooner or later appreciate his generosity and time will change him. A crook, however, will make false stories, provoke the mob to go along with him, and use all other means to attack a gentleman immediately and ruthlessly. This is why a gentleman often fails when he deals with a crook.

A gentleman would rather hold his doctrines than to win a game, and withdraw from an unfair competition. Quite differently, the only precept of a crook is to win, win, and win, fairly or unfairly. When necessary, the latter will maneuver all available devices to attain his aims.

A gentleman is pleased to see the success and prosperity of others. He will motivate people by recognizing in public the strengths and special talents of others. In sharp contrast, a malicious person will be glad to see the fall of the world. He will search from all possible sources, such as in the private life, personal conversation, or published works to find flaws, errors, and imperfections, and employ them to attack his targeted individuals.

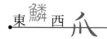

There is a clear distinction of justice from greed. Those who always assert justice and live up with the laws of righteousness are no doubt gentlemen. Those who often play crafts for the purpose of gaining their personal attainments are certainly shrewd persons.

To a gentleman, all people around him are gentlemen. He knows how to restraint himself, and is often tolerant and sympathetic of others for their behaviors. To a wicked person, all people are sick. He is always mean, demanding, and self-centered.

A gentleman will be better to achieve his service goals in an environment where laws are in perfect order, governments are highly effective, and people are enlightened, well informed, and respected. A crook, however, will mostly gain his ground and succeed in a chaotic world where laws are despiteful, governments are corrupted, and people are illiterate, uninformed, and ignorant.

TO BE HAPPY

Many rich men have unlimited wealth, drive Mercedez Benzes, own luxurious resorts, and enjoy extravagant lives. Many poor people have to walk with their thin legs under burning sunshine, sleep in subway tunnels or outdoor places even during freezing winter, and sweat or even risk their lives only to survive. The rich is not necessary smarter than the poor, and the poor is not always inferior to the rich.

Many people are mayors, governors, presidents, military commanders, or business executives, who have power to give orders and authority to enjoy their prestige. Many others are clerks, front line staff, or lower rank of employees, who have to stay in the positions for life, labor day and night, and bend their backbones to the bosses only to earn a pitiful living. The bosses are not necessary great; they may be only vulgarians. The subordinates are not always common people; they may be intelligent, capable, and intellectual geniuses.

All men and women die; no matter they are rich or poor, prestigious or humble. But some die young and

others live many years longer. Many died young are good, decent, and honorable friends, relatives, sisters, or brothers. Some evils, killers, and tyrants should not have been born to the world at first, and they often live on and on, and live much longer than the world could bear upon.

Fair or in despair, this is the world, where many events are out of human hands. No one can control a family or a place where he wants to be born. No one can be certain when the wheel of fortune would stop or whether or not he would win a jackpot at gambling. One becomes wealthy or prosperous often just because he grabs a right opportunity at the right time and the right place. One's efforts could be in vain or in drain if he misses one of these right events. Believe it or not, the super-nature or God is the architect of the universe; and it seems that circumstance or fate often determines one's material world.

Nevertheless, one should not be discouraged because it seems that the world is foredoomed. One has to recognize that God creates the world, but also grants ample room for men to exercise their free wills. No one has ever sensed the form, color, or taste of fate, which might be only a myth that men create to justify failures.

One is encouraged to seek the advice from his religious teachers when he is in confusion, dilemma, or trouble. One may read horoscopes or see fortune-tellers occasionally for relaxing. One should never be further confused, however, by those words of prophets. No diviners or magicians are God or could read the mind of God. All of them are nothing but human beings, who are even not able to tell what will happen to themselves.

Be alert that people fall preys to wilful prophets when they are weak, lost, and frightened in darkness where they are uncertain of their future. James Baker, a TV evangelist, once cheated in the name of God a great deal of fortune by taking advantage of the simple mind of people. In many Asian towns and cities, temples are built to collect money and make profits. Why do fortune-tellers have to remain as fortune-tellers if they are able to tell fortune correctly?

One ought to have faith in God, but also needs to have confidence of his own will that is granted by Him. One shall never be serious about the message delivered by any fate or fortune-tellers. The world will be deadly dead if men and women all believe their fates are doomed. Fortunately, the frontiers of civilization are always

broadening and the world is continuously moving forward
only because most people have ignored fatalism.

Provided by Prof. Brian L. Millholf

All living animals have to labor to survive. Working
bees have to travel far under sunshine or storm to gather
nectar and pollen for food and honeycombs. Many of them
are killed on their ways of hard and busy working either by
the strike of storms or by the traps of spiders. Men, too,
are born to work for meals, shelters, and entertainments.
But with conscious minds, men are always striving to
improve their environment so that they can live better and

better.

Achilles, hero in Homer's *Iliad,* never stopped fighting when he was challenged although he had a fatal heel. Captain Ahab, hero in Melville's *Moby Dick,* was crippled and killed at the end of his chase after the white whale over high seas. After a long struggle over the risky ocean, the old man in Hemingway's story pulled ashore only the skeleton of a big fish.

The meaning of these stories lay not in the emptiness at the end, but in the long and entire course of continuous adventures, one after another, during the expeditions. In the stories, none of the heroes acquiesced that life was predetermined and inevitable. On the contrary, they displayed their courage, persistence, and best efforts in quest of their destinations. It was the hardships and risks that made their lives active, exciting, challenging, and full of meaning. It was the overcoming their risks and the conquest of their hardships that made them heroes who were accomplishing, fulfilling, and satisfying.

Helen A. Keller became an unusual historical figure because she strived hard to learn, write, and lecture. She faced but never yielded to the difficult reality of brain

damage, that caused her both blind and deaf in her entire life. Jesus showed no fear to the thorns, bleeding, and cruelty of Crucifixion that led to the birth of Christianity. The Crucifixion also signified resurrection to the world.

These and many other stories present examples reminding us that the value of life is not necessary to gain the fragile and earthly materials or to hold the temporary and delusive positions or titles. Being born to the world, one, however, has to commit to a destiny, continuously take challenges, and persistently act one's best to fulfil his obligations. He himself is the one who mostly directs the course of his journey towards the end of life.

Discontentment with what one has had, jealousy of others for what they have owned, and greed for those that one does not deserve to have will only lead one to an unhappy and miserable life. One certainly will live more content when he has full faith in God, thorough understanding the meaning of life, and tries his best with what he is granted in his life. One may complain about something that he is crazed about and does not have it, but he would appreciate it if he could look around himself and realize many other things he is bestowed.

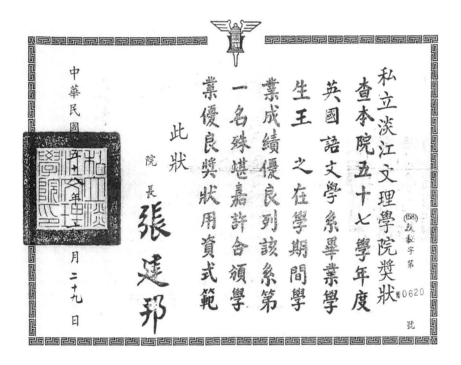

University of Pittsburgh

To all persons to whom these presents may come, Greeting
Be it known that

Chih Wang

having satisfied the requirements for the degree of

Doctor of Philosophy

and having been recommended by the Graduate Faculty in

The School of Library and Information Science

is now admitted to that degree with all the rights, privileges and
immunities thereunto appertaining.

In Witness Thereof, we the Trustees of the University have caused
our corporate seal and the proper signatures to be hereunto affixed.

Given at Pittsburgh, Pennsylvania on the seventeenth day of December in
the year of our Lord one thousand nine hundred and eighty-eight.

Chairman, Board of Trustees

Provost

Wesley W. Posvar
President

Toni Carbo Bearman
Dean, School of Library and Information Science

210

一九九〇年關島總督圖資大會計劃工作組合照

一九九一年白宮圖資大會關島代表合照於華盛頓會場

University of Guam Robert F. Kennedy Memorial Library Groundbreaking
Ceremony, Aug. 24, 1990: L-R: Congressman Ben G. Blaz; Dr. Chih Wang,
Dean of Learning Resources; Dr. Rosa R. Carter, former President,
University of Guam; Governor Joseph F. Ada; Dr. Wilfred P. Leon Guerrero,
President, University of Guam, and other Guam dignities not shown in the
picture. About $8 million have been appropriated by the government of
Guam for renovating and expanding the R. F. K. Memorial Library.

一九九〇年關島大學新建圖書館破土典禮
總督、國會議員等主持

沙士 SARS 與國家安全

生物病菌侵襲，疾病發軔之初，有一段潛伏的時期，在此期間，沒有任何疾病的現象。起初，一些兒童、老年、愛死病患，以及接受化療、身体抗疫能力薄弱的人，開始發病。他們受生物病菌的侵害，以為感冒傳染，照常尋求一般醫生診治。醫生也以一般病例處方，沒有特別警覺，沒有注意病患人數增加。於是，疾病開始傳染，病患的家人和親友，受到了感染。

病患愈傳愈多，病況愈益嚴重，醫生之間開始互相通報，并向衛生機構報案。經由各地疾病檢查實驗室，亞城的疾病管制中心 CDC，終於收到病菌的抽樣。經過檢驗，判定抽樣的生物菌，為天花的變種病毒。

病毒確定時，實際已與第一批病患發病的時間，相去甚久。因此，疾病早已擴散，各醫院已擠滿病患，和許多疑似感染病毒的人。醫院的病床和醫療器材，出現了短缺的現像；各地的醫護人員，開始屯聚藥品。抗菌藥物，空運到了疫區，卻因分送配套設施不夠完備，無法送到病患大眾。由於病毒急速爆發，CDC 和公共衛生人員，疲於奔命，無法追查疾病的來源。同時，因抗菌試驗藥品的應用，也產生了許多意想不到的問題，諸如使用試驗藥物，如何獲得病患同意；大量處方，特別是應用於靜脈注射，如何處理等等。

設法控制疾病流行，為大家共識的優先工作，但公共衛生機構和醫療社團，卻意見紛歧，不能合作。衛生機構則因工作忙亂，通信設備老舊，彼此失去了溝通和聯系。政府雖有多種政策和法令，治安機關、衛生單位、地方政府，以及緊急救難人員，卻不韻熟，遇事都要臨時商討決定。

疾病擴散以後，各種人力資源隨之短缺，進而危及電信、電力和交通管制等影響重大的供應和服務。疾病的快速漫延，使得政府考慮採取區域隔離，以為防護的措施。各地方、各機構失去了統一的行政系統，指揮、控制，和彼此的交通聯系，各自為政，各行其是，陣腳大亂。

最後終於有了一套隔離措施，但為時晚矣。衛生、治安、以及緊急救難人員，沒有演訓，對於新的措施，毫無準備。衛生機構執行隔離政策，處置失當，而引起附近民眾的恐慌，大批逃離。鄰近各州的居民，更因害怕而反彈，迫使州政府出動自衛隊，防堵感染區逃來的民眾。離家逃亡的民眾，進不得，又不願退回自己的家園，而陷於進退維谷的困境；於是，社會秩序大亂。

近代以來，美國成了唯一獨尊的超強，俾倪世界；不論軍政、財經和科技，沒有國家，可與倫比。或因如此，卻成了恐怖份子的對象，國內國外，不斷受到攻擊破壞；最近，紐約、華府，國家心腹，五角大廈，軍事中樞，竟遭重大攻擊；白宮咫尺之隔，受到威脅，僅僅倖免於難而已。

鑒於恐怖份子不斷的攻擊，美國朝野，早已有了各種各樣的策略和行動。其中，民間智庫策略和萬國研究中心 Center for Strategic and International Studies（CSIS），於二○○○年前後，即已草擬《對抗生化、放射物，和核子恐怖攻擊 *Combating Chemical, Biological, Radiological, and Nuclear Terrorism*（CBRN）》一書 （CSIS, 2001）。本文前段，為摘譯該書當中，假設狀況，描述受到生物菌攻擊以後發生的情景。

時間相去三數年，沙士發生於大陸、港臺，前後對照，各地情節，猶如翻版覆製。後者更勞命傷財，感染病死許多人民生命，嚴重損害人民財產，衝擊國家經濟。政府當局若能警覺，未雨綢繆，早有防備措施，即使抄襲外人的「前車之鑑」，碰到沙士來襲，當可從容應付，即時予以隔離、消毒、診治；而減少枉死生命，減低國家和人民的無謂損失。

沙士侵襲以後，根據初步研究報導，認為沙士病毒，來自動物。老廣同胞，嗜食野味，沙士早期病例，發生於廣東，其中關聯，自有蛛絲馬跡。據說，大陸電子網路，另有耳語意見，懷疑沙士大難，為西方國家撒了野。這種傳言，大抵為民族主義的情緒發洩，趁機嫁禍。

不過，回顧歷史，中國民間的疑竇，也非毫無背景。成吉思汗不僅彎弓射大鵰，畢竟曾征服歐亞，而成為西方世界的黃禍；無獨有偶，英文裡還創造了一個蒙古病症。毛澤東瘋狂，韓戰、越戰、大鬧世界革命，把天下搞得天翻地覆，驚動了西方強權。最近，亞洲出現四小龍，又說，二十一世紀為華人天下。世界強權爭霸，一山難容二虎，偏激狂人，思前顧後，有心破壞，在華人天下，放點病毒，衡情度理，不是完全沒有可能。

需知，恐怖狂暴之徒，不僅出沒於阿富汗、伊拉克等美國國務院列名的國家；歐美、日本，都有土生土長的極端份子。美國的三K黨，白人至上，不容有色人種；奧克拉荷馬市內，聯邦大廈被炸，東京地鐵放毒害人，都是美日本土恐怖份子所幹的暴行。

　　恐怖暴行，有出於某些特定國家或組織；也有恐怖狂徒，因信邪中毒，或政治思想偏狹，或神經錯亂失常，挺而走險，幹出了狂妄的行動。此次沙士，由大陸爆發，散佈於港臺等華人地區，以普通代數的消去法，或以代爾法 Delphi 判斷，二者之中，非甲即乙；不是自然發生傳染，便是恐怖暴徒或組織，偷雞摸狗，放了生物病菌。

　　恐怖暴徒處心積慮，時時放火，處處施暴，令人疲於奔命，防不勝防。美國超強，面臨恐怖份子的攻擊破壞，已經檢討又檢討，訂出了種種策略和措施，以保護國家安全，電子空間 cyberspace 暢通無阻。經過了沙士的突發衝擊，中華民國國家安全、社會治安等有關才智賢達，不知有沒有深入探討，詳細研究沙士可能的原始來源，並亡羊補牢，提出可行措施，防範類似重大緊急事件，如生化、放射物、核子等，或天災、或人禍的恐怖攻擊，再度暴發；以確實保護國家安全、經濟持續發展、和人民的生命財產？

香港回歸

七月一日到了，香港終於回歸中國！身為世界重鎮，亞洲貿易、運輸、通信、金融，及觀光的樞紐，香港的回歸，不僅是中國和香港的大事，也成了全世界注意力的焦點。

香港於一八四一年，因鴉片戰爭，清庭戰敗，為大英帝國強行攫取。一九四五年二次大戰之後，中國曾有機會收回香港，但因內部戰亂而作罷。一九八四年，英國與中共獲得協議，同意香港於九七年回歸，條件是維持香港現行政治體制五十年。

香港位於廣東海岸，共有二三六個大小島嶼，面積約為一、○二七平方公里，分為九龍、香港、新界、外島四區。人口約六百三十萬，主要聚居於港九及新界。

回歸之前，香港數百萬的居民，已經移居歐美和大洋洲各國，或在各地取得了居留證。許多大企業和大量資金，也已外移。按常理，香港的政權移交，將不致引起混亂和不安，對於世界各地商務和生活，也不致有重大影響。

根據網際網絡的調查，香港回歸之後，最值得注意的為香港的政治民主、經濟發展和新聞自由等問題。惟一般相信，今日的中共領導，多為聰明理智、通達時務的人士。因此預期並希望，香港回歸中國之後，他們會信守諾言，保證一國兩制、港人治港的政策，並維持香港社會安定、經濟繁榮的現狀。理由很簡單，中共領導必須向世界昭示，他們遵守國際條約，共產中國為國際團體的禮義之邦。他們尤須向台灣顯示，中國可行一國兩制。

香港回歸，為中國長久的願望，但為時拖延了半個世紀，對於中華民國政府而言，為極大的遺憾。中華民國政府領導軍民，與盟國並肩作戰，流血犧牲，最後打敗日本，贏得了二次大戰。香港若於戰後、一九四五年歸還中國，是中華民國政府莫大的勝利。五十年之後，中華民國退守侷居於臺灣一隅，而香港卻歸還其敵手中共政權。形勢所迫，臺灣方面只好「戒急用忍」，笑著臉吞下苦澀的現實了。

而且繼香港之後，澳門即將歸還。待港澳塵埃落定，中共勢必矛頭指向台灣，高舉民族主義大旗，高喊國家主權和領土統一，加強政治、外交、和軍事壓力，強迫統一臺灣。但若台灣內部能夠穩定堅強，外加國際之間，必須考慮平衡勢力，港澳歸還之後，台海兩岸的現狀，或者仍能維持一段時間。

HONG KONG'S TURNOVER TO CHINA

Hong Kong is going to return to China on July 1. As it is one of the most important trading, transportation, communications, financial, and tourist centers of the world, the turnover of Hong Kong will be not only a great historical event in China and Hong Kong, but also has become the focal attention and concern of the entire world.

Hong Kong was an integrated part of China until 1841, when it was taken by the British Empire through a forced treaty after the later defeated China in the dirty Opium War. It would have returned in 1945 if there were no internal turmoil in China after World War II. The British Empire and China signed an accord in 1984 to transfer Hong Kong back to China in 1997 on the condition that Hong Kong will maintain as a separate political and social system for another 50 year.

Lying at the east coast of Canton, a province of China, Hong Kong comprises of 236 islands, covering a land space of over 1,000 sq. km. It is divided into four major districts: Kowloon, Hong Kong Island, the New

Territories, and the Outlying Islands. There are about six million people, 98% being Chinese, living mostly in the first three districts.

Thousands of Hong Kong's residents have moved to or secured residential status in, and large number of businesses and significant amount of capital have been relocated to, American, European, and Oceanian countries during the years when the turnover is approaching. The imminent transfer would not cause further complications and turbulence, and would not have an immediate and dramatic impact on the business and the life of the world.

An ongoing Internet survey of Chinese language readers indicates that democracy, economy, and freedom of journalism, among other things, are the major concerns after Hong Kong is turned over. It is believed, nevertheless, that today's Communist leaders are knowledgeable, reasonable, and practical. They will, hopefully, let Hong Kong maintain status quo, stable, and prosperous at least in a foreseeable future when it is handed over to China. They need to affirm that they observe the signed accord, demonstrate that China is a civil member of the world community, and show deliberately to the people on Taiwan that their policy of one-country two systems（socialism and capitalism）will work.

To the Republic of China on Taiwan, the turnover will apparently be an embarrassment and a dilemma. As one of the major alliances that won World War II, it would be a great triumph of the government if Hong Kong returned to China immediately after the war. ROC has retreated to Taiwan since 1949, and now Hong Kong is to be handed over to the Communist China, an ROC's rival regime. ROC cannot but swallow the bitter reality of the turnover.

After Hong Kong, Macao will soon be back to China. Taiwan will then be the only significant Chinese territory that separates from China. On the ground of national integrity, sovereignty, and pride, Communist China will certainly turn to Taiwan as its target of unification after Hong Kong and Macao return. It will definitely increase its diplomatic, political, and military pressure on Taiwan. Hopefully, the status quo along the Taiwan strait will be maintained at least in the near future because of the need of power balance in the world.

TO INVEST IN UNIVERSITY OF GUAM

It seems that Governor Carl Gutierrez does have a vision for the future of Guam and has tried to push for the realization of it. One of his first actions after he took office was to take an Asian trip to solicit foreign investment and particularly to build new hotels on Guam. With aggressive goals in mind, he is attempting to stimulate another economic miracle on island, which may surpass the previous boom.

While looking the outside world for investment, Governor Gutierrez and his management team ought not to overlook Guam's own assets in sustaining island economy. The University of Guam （UOG） is one of these viable and vital resources. While hotels are critical to attract Asian tourists and generate revenues, UOG draws approximately 4,000 students from all over the world.

Assuming that each of these students spends $25,000 a year in average, UOG would bring $100 million to the island each year. These students are not seasonable, fluctuant, and short-term tourists. Most of them stay at

UOG for four, five, or six years. An indigenous student would spend more than $25,000 a year at other colleges and universities off island if Guam does not have a university that would add up a huge sum of loss for the island.

Among the 4000 students, at least one-thirds of them are none local residents. The friends and family members of these students naturally become frequent visitors of Guam and would make a large sum contribution to the island economy. Besides, UOG offers various programs in Micronesia and other locations, which enrol additional 1000 or more students, who bring in extra monies to Guam each year. As a U.S. land grant university, UOG also receives funds from U.S. Federal government and other foundations. These funds are pumped into Guam economy annually.

While hotels are pivotal to Guam economy and tax revenues, all major hotels on Guam are controlled by off-islands owners, and the primary portion of their profits is transferred off shore. While the total revenues of UOG might be smaller than those created by hotels and other businesses, most of the over $100 million of UOG annual

incomes remain and are spent on Guam.

We all are familiar with the term of U.S. education export. We all know the reality of many "college towns" in the U.S. mainland, where higher education is the only local business. Guam is a small island. The income of over $100 million a year is not a small business.

If UOG is bankrupted, how the Government of Guam is going to deal with about 600 competent professionals at the University? How would it affect island businesses and economy? Would Guam be worse than the Subic Bay of the Philippines after U.S. military installations were moved out several years ago? Would Guam become another ghost town similar to those seen in the U.S. mainland? The UOG's vitality would be easily discernible when we pause a second to imagine what it would happen if there is not a UOG to bring in over $100 million a year for Guam.

More important than a hotel facility, UOG especially has a mission to provide higher education to people on Guam and throughout Micronesia. It is understood that education is a long-term investment. Monies invested in education will have returns in the long run, and the return will depend upon the amount of investment. It is certain that if there is no investment, there will have no return.

Fifty years ago after World War II, Japan was destroyed to the ground. Twenty or so years ago, Hong Kong, Singapore, South Korea, and Taiwan were poor. Today, Japan has become an economic power. The others are the "four little economic dragons" in Asia. How did they do it? They all invested annually a great sum of their national incomes in education. They are now enjoying the fruitful returns of their investment.

For a huge sum of short-term revenues, for the continuing growth of Guam, for long term returns, and for education of young men and women on island and throughout Micronesia, Guam political leaders, executives and legislators need to re-review their priorities and find a way, from public revenues and / or private giving, to fund UOG adequately; particularly to fund sufficiently UOG Library, that is the core of teaching, learning, research, and services of the University.

If Government of Guam could not afford UOG financially, UOG should be privatised. For many years, Asian entrepreneurs have been ready to buy the Pentagon and even the White House. If people of Guam are willing to

accept it, Asian corporations might be interested in buying UOG.

To support education, UOG, and libraries is always a bipartisan matter. To fund UOG, particularly its main library, appropriately, and to help the University maintain its academic standards, pursue further growth and development, and quest for excellence at this difficult time would be especially notable to over 10,000 students, faculty, staff, friends, and family members of UOG community. To invest in the University of Guam now, we certainly will have fruitful returns in the future. Over 10,000 members of UOG community are closely watching government activities; their voices and votes will make things quite different.

UNIVERSITY OF GUAM MADE PROGRESS

Recently, several commentaries about the University of Guam （UOG） appeared in the *Pacific Daily News*. It is a positive sign that the University has drawn attention and become a focal point of the island community. This is a response to comments made by Daljit Singh.

The University has made tremendous progress in recent years. The new buildings for the University Library, the Micronesian Area Research Center, and the Computer Center were dedicated a few weeks ago. A physical master plan to build and restructure the entire campus was presented. And a campaign to raise funds to implement the plan is well under way and has received many positive responses.

Many new academic programs including an off-campus institute in Japan has been initiated. The Computer Center is planning a campus network. The University Library has immediate access to the national Dialog system, Online Computer Library Center （OCLC）, Bitnet, Internet, and other electronic networks. It also has

contracted with Dec / Dynix for an automation system, which will be the foundation for linking the University with other parts of the world.

Dialog has over 350 subject databases including many business reference sources. OCLC has over 11,000 participating libraries with more than 25 million bibliographic records. Networks immediately connect UOG with hundreds of other universities on the U.S. mainland for information and interlibrary loans（ILLs）. In-house library materials are important. The fact is that no library can hold everything in today's world. The concept of access has, therefore, outweighed the necessity to own every bit of information. ILLs and faxing have long been a practice in libraries to support the needs of research.

Nicholas Goetzfridt recently published an award-winning book entitled *Indigenous Navigation and Voyaging in the Pacific*. He annotated in detail 700 works published in English, German, Chinese, and Japanese; no more than 30 percent of these works were located on Guam.

This writer and other faculty at UOG have kept on publishing articles in top journals. An intellectual who complains of inadequate resources on hand for his lack of research is just like a high school dropout who blames insufficient support at home for his schoolwork.

Not long ago, three new deans were recruited to UOG from Georgia. None of them knew Jimmy Carter nor were they acquainted with Governor Ada before they came to Guam. Singh himself once was a significant administrator at UOG. No evidence indicates that he was placed in the position because of his political kinship. Politics and bureaucracy are common in different environments. These activities at UOG might not be worse than those at other situations.

UOG is located on a remote island and is a small, open door institution with regional missions. It is not situated in Cambridge or New England, where one has the convenience of physical contact with seemingly endless resources. It is ridiculous to hear him complaining about UOG, which he chose as his long-term home. It is outrageous that he did not feel his share of responsibilities for the non-accredited status of the College of Business and Public Administration programs and other negligence at the university in the past.

Singh also ought to be legally liable when he publicly accuses students of cheating without any evidence. Besides, it is the duty of instructors to control classroom activities. If students in his classes cheated, Singh and not anyone else should take responsibility.

International students flooded into the prestigious Ivy League institutions, Berkeley, and other known universities because of their names. These students also promoted the academic achievements and image of these institutions. For fulfilling its regional missions and future development, UOG needs international students.

One might not see anything in the world when he buries his head in the sands. A "scholar" who seldom goes to libraries will not see and understand the available computer and print resources when he does not do "serious" research. UOG and its library belong to the faculty, students, and the community. Each individual of the community has a share of responsibility to help the University and its library grow. One does not have much to say about them if he does not have any positive input to these institutions.

RATING OF UNIVERSITY OF GUAM

J. C. Salas, Academic Vice President at the University of Guam （UOG）, reported in the *Pacific Daily News* （August 7, 1992, p. 3） that the University "is on an upward trend" and that its rating in the academic world "would be better" if it were redone today. His statement was made in response to the Gourman Report published in 1987, in which UOG was marginally rated 2.88 in a scale of 1 to 5.

Salas was right in that the University has made great progress in many aspects. The University Library alone has changed rapidly in the recent years. Within three months, when the renovation of the building is completed, the Library will occupy a new facility with its physical size almost being doubled to 54,000 square feet. About $400,000 of equipment for a library automation system has arrived. Installation and training are underway.

The Library has linked with major library and information systems providing instant access to over 350 information databases and 13,000 libraries worldwide for online cataloging, reference searching, and interlibrary

loans. It has acquired 12 CD-ROMs for quick reference and U.S. government information. Its proposed acquisitions budget for 1993 will increase 500 percent in comparison to that of 1989, although much more will be needed in the future.

More importantly, the University Library has a harmonious team of dedicated, highly qualified, and self-motivated faculty and staff. In addition to routine library services, the Library has sponsored several important workshops and conferences to serve library and information professionals on Guam and throughout Micronesia. The faculty members have been very active in leading and presenting papers in the activities of local, national, and international professional organizations. They have been highly productive in research and publishing. All these great events have occurred within a short period of about three years, which does not happen quite often to many colleges and universities in the world.

By the progress made in the Library in recent years alone, it is evident that any assessment done three years ago is invalid in measuring the University of today. Furthermore, note that Gourman has published over 10 books ranking colleges and universities. One study, however, revealed that all Gourman's books contain numerous inexcusable flaws, are worthless, and "virtually without merit." (*RQ.* Spring, 1986. pp. 323-330) .

It is no question that the University needs to do much more to promote its academic status and image. However, no matter for any reason, one continuously complain, cry wolf, and attack the University will not help improve the institution. Worse than that any attack with personal purposes will certainly undermine the credibility, personality, and ethics of the individual attacker.

There are various ways and means to promote the image and raise the academic rating of the University. For individual faculty, one positive action is to engage in rigorous research, produce refereed publications, and present quality papers in scholarly conferences. After a certain time, the collective results of these productive activities will surely help the University gain recognition in the academic world. The scholar and professional works will also enhance the visibility and marketability of individuals in the widely open society.

中國人的月亮

朔： 　農曆初一的月。朔，迎接新月回來之意。

朏： 　初三新現、但光亮不足之月。英文為
　　　crescent，意為成長之月，土耳其以為其國
　　　旗之圖案，也有取成長之意。

明： 　初四、五以後漸次明亮的月。

望： 　十五之滿月 full moon。太陽、地球、月
　　　亮同在一條線上，日在東，月在西，互相遙
　　　「望」。

魄： 　十六日以後，月所生的陰影。

晦： 　月終之日，即沒有月光的暗夜。

上弦月： 初七、八，月上缺，如弓弦向上。

下弦月： 二十四、五，月下缺，似弓弦向下。

新月： 　初三、四、五之月。

殘月： 　望後漸漸暗淡下去的月。

九九俚歌

　　中國自梁朝起，民間即傳有九九俚歌，從冬至
交九為始，以數九計算冬去春來，農民下田耕作的時
機： 一九、二九，伸不出手；三九、四九，凍死貓
狗；五九、六九，隔河看柳；七九河開；八九雁來；
九九寒盡，春暖花開。

閑 讀 抄 摘

Reading and Reviews

DILBERT'S SALARY THEOREM

Librarians and professors will never make as much as business executives, salespersons, administrators, or lawyers. The theorem is supported by the following mathematical equation:

We know that knowledge is power, i.e.,

knowledge = power;

and time is money, i.e.,

time = money.

We also know that,

power = work / time.

Now, substitute power with knowledge and time with money, the equation becomes,

knowledge = work / money.

To obtain the amount of money, the equation can be as: money = work / knowledge.

We then can see that when you have more knowledge, your money will be less. When your knowledge approaches zero, your money becomes infinite regardless how much work you have done.

看《毛澤東和他的女人們》

這是一本好書，必須一看。

作者京夫子通過毛澤東生平與許許多多女人的非常關係，翔實生動地敘述了毛共高層之間鬥爭奪權的血腥內幕。

毛澤東粗俗地說：「蘿蔔拔掉眼還在」，他認為男女間事，如雞如狗，不過如此而已。因之，他的專列火車，巡遊南北，所到之處，即興播種，蘿蔔窩無所不在。毛好跳舞游泳，其舞池、泳池之旁，必有床蓆，供他興之所至，隨時休息使用。

毛澤東進了紫禁城，不僅成了新皇帝，更成了超神。全國青年男女，瘋狂崇拜，莫不以奉獻身體，服務偉大領袖為一生榮幸。因此，毛澤東雖無後宮，卻可隨時隨地，任意挑選千嬌百媚，盡享國色天香。本書羅列有名有姓，與毛澤東有親密關係的女人有：楊開慧、賀子貞、江青、張毓鳳、陶斯詠、吳廣惠、馮鳳鳴、孫維世、上官雲珠、白玉蓮等等。其他未見經傳，與毛一夕風流，沾有龍種的女人，為數何止三千。

毛澤東不但善舞好色，更嗜殺人。從井崗山，到陝北窰洞，再進紫禁城，一路整風、三反、五反、大

躍進、文化大革命的血腥運動，加上和國民黨的激烈
戰爭，抗美援朝，被驅迫、被屠殺的善良人民，何止
千千萬萬；即在大躍進，文化大革命時期，被飢餓、
被折磨而死的人民，便有六、七千萬人（臺澎地區現
在不過二千三百萬人）。

　　毛澤東尤善權術，猜忌成性，手段陰險狠毒，不
但屠殺國特，屠殺善良無辜，也設盡方法，逼迫、折
磨、酷虐和殺害與他一起做土匪、革命起家的伙件。
其中受害較為著名的計有：王明、張國燾、李立三、
瞿秋白、張聞天、秦邦憲、彭德懷、賀龍、羅瑞卿、
劉少奇、林彪等等。

　　彭德懷曾三度救了毛的生命，帶領抗美援朝戰
爭；劉少奇曾創毛澤東思想，為國家主席；林彪帶領
四野，從東北打到南方，為毛的親密戰友，革命接班
人，都逃脫不了毛的魔掌，被他暗算、折磨、殺害。

　　周恩來和劉、彭、賀、林等共黨革命元勳，忠
心耿耿，為毛爭奪天下，建立紅色帝國，功勳蓋天，
看他們可憐可悲的淒慘下場，不免令人同情憐憫。
其實，他們也是大魔鬼，是毛澤東屠殺千千萬萬中國
人民的幫兇，他們被折磨、被害、被殺，也是老天有
眼，罪有應得。

　　毛好《金瓶梅》，套了潘金蓮的話說：「人死

臭塊地。」只是他這個好色之徒，忘恩負義，殘害忠狗，屠殺千千萬萬的善良人民，罪惡昭彰，為什麼他的臭皮囊，時至今日，還要供放在天安門廣場？

鐵幕緊閉的時候，海峽兩岸，各說各話，說大陸同胞吃草根、樹皮、觀音土，餓莩遍野；臺灣人民啃香蕉皮。鐵幕打開以後，真話假話，一清二楚，只是台灣說得有欠具體。不要先入為主，笑京夫子寫反共八股，故意找渣，懷疑書中的報導。須知毛澤東的陰謀陽謀，他是任何傷天害理的壞事都幹得出來的。

近日，古華先生為紀念吳祖光夫婦，撰寫了一篇「曠代才子佳人」（中副網路版 5/8/03）。吳夫婦為中國劇藝界名家。古文提到，本篇推介的大作，洛陽紙貴，在北京暗底流通傳閱；而吳先生早於一九九九年，即在中共政協討論會中，嚴正質詢：「天安門城樓上那個王八蛋的畫像，為甚麼還不搞下，還讓他繼續在那裡欺騙、愚弄人民？」（原文照錄。）

吳先生夫婦，哲人已逝，但吳先生如雷呼聲，震聾發聵，猶在空谷迴盪，正是筆者積悶在心的大疑問，更是千千萬萬中國人民內心的共鳴。吳先生嘗

了老虎膽，敢於半閉半開的鐵幕之內，在京戲禁宮、
紅色廟堂中，震破天空，大聲高呼；視死如歸，朝聞
道，千萬人頭落地，吾往矣；氣慨萬千，無愧為中國
傳統的士人大儒，通達義理的現代智識分子了！

KNOWLEDGE WORKERS

— Peter E. Drucker

Knowledge cannot be productive unless the
knowledge worker finds out who he is himself, what kinds
of work he is fitted for, and how he works best.

The knowledge worker… is not productive under the
spur of fear; only self-motivation and self-direction can
make him productive.

The knowledge worker--No one can motivate him.
He has to motivate himself. No one can direct him. He
has to direct himself. No one can supervise him. He is the
guardian of his own standards, of his own performance,
and of his own objectives. He can be productive only if he
is responsible for his own job.

中國歷史的血肉見證

—讀無名氏名著《紅鯊》

　　一九六五年，大作家索辛尼辛出版了《吉拉格群島》，以親身經歷，加上兩百多人身歷其境的事實，揭露蘇俄暴政的歷史，驚動了全世界。一九八九年，有名的無名氏發表了《紅鯊》，以萬死一生的經歷，細述中國共產黨的勞改營，以聞所未聞，慘無人道的手段，迫害和殘殺你我的父老同胞。書出之後，震憾全球。

　　聽過井底牢沒有？二十餘米深，直徑二米，面積不到一個塌塌米，井口有蓋，上了鐵鎖，有小通氣孔。沒有光線，沒有足夠的空氣，沒有聲音，沒有時間，每天一點稀漿糊，在裡頭吃、睡、坐、尿、屎，拘留五百四十天，能忍受嗎？

　　青藏公路又叫亡魂谷、堆屍溝、血之路、淚之橋，為什麼？看，天寒地凍，冰天雪地，攝氏零下二十度，抬頭是高山峻嶺，腳下是千丈溝壑，人似壁虎，附貼於懸崖峭壁，槍尖環伺之下，用手用十字鎬，開山鋪路，轟然一聲，大石小石，沙土樹桿，隆隆滾下；勞改犯人，你我的父老同胞，血肉橫飛，粉身碎骨，頃刻之間，由半山墜下谷底深淵。

一天三雞（饑），人鳥，食屍獸，又是什麼？勞改犯人，你我的父老同胞，曾苦苦於糞便中覓食，相信嗎？

你我都看到，六四慘案，人民解放軍以機槍和坦克，血腥解放無數的人民。但我們曾聽說過一九五九年至一九六一年間，青海柴達木盆地的勞改犯，你我的父老同胞，被餓死、凍死、槍斃了十幾萬人 — 幾乎等於關島老小的全部人口；一九六八年，西寧造反無理，被人民解放軍以機槍、手榴彈，解放歸天了近萬人民嗎？

《紅鯊》，四六八頁，由井底牢、紅鯊、提籃颱嘯、柴達木風情畫，荒漠裡的人、帕米爾的秘密、和毛澤東死的那天數篇，一氣呵成，為中國近代的歷史，作有血有肉的見證。史實和描述，動人肺腑。讀官若生活無聊，正好三缺一，或在蔣家長李家短，不妨看看《紅鯊》，但務請準備手帕，為看到傷心不忍之處使用。

軍閥、偽滿、毛皇朝

─ 簡介《鴻》一書

　　二十世紀以來，中國多災多亂。中山先生領導革命，推翻專制腐敗的滿清皇朝之後，曹、吳、馮、孫、袁等軍閥，群雄割據，互相殘殺征閥。國民革命興起，南征北戰，國家未及統一，日本帝國傾巢入侵，夾其強大國勢，蠶食鯨吞中國。二次大戰之後，中國國弱民貧，未稍喘息，共產黨受到蘇俄的野心卵翼，又起兵作亂，赤化了大陸。接著是抗美援朝、三反五反、大煉鋼、大躍進、人民公社、文化大革命、紅衛兵等，一而再，再而三的運動，中國天翻地覆，不得一時一刻的和平寧靜。

　　《鴻：三代中國女人的故事》，就是張戎，小名二鴻，以她自己，母親德鴻及姥姥三代的經歷，敘述這個多災多亂的世代中，苦難的中國人民所遭受的各種各樣、大大小小的災亂和折磨。

　　張的姥姥出生於清末，成長於民初，正逢內有革命戰爭，軍閥割據，外有列強侵略，割地賠款，中國社會動盪不安，民窮財盡。為了巴結攀附，提高地位，改善生活，張的姥姥於十五歲稚齡，被出賣給軍閻作小妾。出嫁之後，新婚三天，便被深鎖於金絲鳥籠，獨守寂寞空閨。

德鴻出生於三〇年代，值日本侵佔東北，成立偽滿。她親身經歷「帝都遙拜」、「天皇遙拜」的日本殖民生活。看過日本皇軍捆綁囚犯，放狗將他們撕成碎片；用刺刀割開人的肚皮，把他們活活劈成兩半的恐佈。她也看到糧食、礦產被運往日本；村莊被燒毀，成千上萬人死亡。

張戎的父親守愚，是共產黨延安時期的老黨員，母親德鴻於一九四七年，年方十五歲時，開始為共產黨地下工作。張出生時，共黨已打下天下，奪得政權，她的父母成了新政權的新貴，共黨的核心高幹，張戎和她的姐弟，是高幹子女，新時代的新寵，享受毛皇朝的特權，哺吸共產黨的乳汁。

毛澤東掀起了一波波的政治運動，迫害人民，囚殺知識份子。像其他共產黨員一樣，張戎的父母和她自己，推波助浪，唯恐不夠積極，不配為毛的信徒。運動偏向，政策錯誤，人民受苦受亂，甚至自己受批鬥，被折磨，他們照樣承受，全部執行，認為那是黨的鞭策和磨練。毛是紅太陽，是上帝，他的話，就是聖旨；他吐口氣，人民不過是螻蟻，財產祇是糞土。

張守愚是不折不扣的老共幹，丟官受辱，被狠批，被毒打，變瘋到死，都是血往肚裡吞，從沒有反黨反毛。其實深陷羅網，待猛然驚醒，他也身不由己，無法無能逃脫魔掌。德鴻是忠貞黨員，瘋狂為黨革命，但並未失去自私的人性。她顧念丈夫，照應兒女；也利用了黨，為家謀利，為張戎鋪路。

張戎和她的姐弟，承襲父母衣缽，是紅色天堂的天使。毛主席指向那裡，他們就奔向那裡，上刀山，下火海，粉身碎骨，在所不惜。但當他們看到除了毛江一夥和半個周恩來之外，千萬的中國人民，共產黨員和幹部，包括他們的父母，手臂被反綁成「噴射飛機」，受到「噴泉」、「風景畫」等奇刑虐待；彭德懷、劉少奇、林彪和陳伯達等親密戰友、國家元首、革命接班人和革命功臣，一一成了修正主義、走資派、工賊和反革命陰謀份子，受到迫害荼毒時，於是反問：如果共產黨的世界是天堂，地獄又是什麼？」

通過三代女人及其周邊人物的大小故事，以東北和四川為主要背景，《鴻》縮影了中國二十世紀的歷史和社會。全書分二十八章，佔四三三頁。除了前面四章共五十五頁之外，全部敘述共產黨革命、鬥爭、毛崇拜、文革、紅衛兵、人民受難、勞改等等。各章之中，並提及纏足、家庭倫理、節慶、民俗等中國傳統文化。

　　本書寫作技巧，對於國民黨，大部份只加公式化的標籤，很少詳述具體細節。對於國民黨的正規軍隊，明顯地表現了很好的印象。共產黨佔據大陸，藉故剷除異己，殺害國民黨遺留人員時，並為辯護：「他們並沒有常常搶東西，也不盡是壞人。」細算起來，國民黨在大陸當政，不過二十年，而且從未統一中國。毛澤東要造反有理，穩固政權，自然醜化敵人，把老軍閥、舊中國、地方勢力和他製造的罪惡，統統加給了國民黨。

　　張戎當過紅衛兵、農民、赤腳醫生、工人等，川大英語系畢業，七八年赴英國研究語言學，九二年得博士學位，為共黨建立政權之後，第一個得到英國博士的大陸同胞，後留英，任教倫敦大學。《鴻》初以英文寫成，名為 Wi ld Swans: Three Daughters of China，曾是暢銷書。中文版由張樸翻譯，譯文通暢甚佳。

CHINA: DECADES OF TURMOIL

Review of *Wild Swans: Three Daughters of
China* by Jung Chang. New York: Simon &
Schuster, 1991. 524 p.

Since the turn of the century, China has been in deep
trouble. From outside, the world powers, including the
European countries, Japan, and Russia, invaded the nation.
Within its own homeland, revolutions and uprisings broke
out all over the country and various factions of warlords
occupied different territories and fiercely fought each
other. Worse than ever, mad Mao engineered one brutal
political campaign after another following the bloodiest
Communist revolution. The nation was torn, devastating,
and paralysed; and people were desperate, despairing, and
groaning.

It is through the stories of three women, Jung Chang,
the author; her mother; and her grandmother, that the
book, *Wild Swans: Three Daughters of China,* depicts
vividly these decades of tumults, upheavals, and tragedies
in China. It is through their disturbing anecdotes that the
book mirrors the pains, sufferings, and desolations of the

Chinese people during these miserable decades.

Jung's grandmother was born at the end of the 19th century. To ameliorate the poverty of her household, to establish a relationship with the officials in Beijing, and to raise the social status of her family, she was traded at 15 by her father to a known warlord as one of his concubines. After enjoyed for three days of ceremony and togetherness, the warlord left her and she was caged in a mansion with endless lonely days.

Her mother, the first swan, grew up in the 1930s, when Japan occupied Manchuria and created its satellite entity to control the region. She witnessed the cruelty of Japanese colonialism, burning down thousands of villages, and shipping out scarce industrial and agricultural products from her hometown to Japan. She saw Japanese soldiers cutting people in half and prisoners tied to stakes being torn to pieces by dogs.

Partially disillusioned by social injustice, foreign invasions, government corruption, and humiliation to the people; and partially enchanted by Maoist exhortations, promises, and propaganda, the first swan swayed to becoming a Communist underground spy when she was

only 15. Later she met and married to her comrade, a
long time Communist veteran. Since then she and her
husband, like many other desolated and enchanted Chinese
youths at the time, worked fanatically and frenetically for
the Communists, wishing that they would bring a hope to
China and its people.

When Jung, the second swan, was born, the
Communists had seized the power and established their
regime in reigning China. She and her brothers and sisters
then became the angels of the Maoist heaven and enjoyed
all kinds of power and privileges that were granted to the
revolutionaries and their families. As it is said, "when a
man gets power, even his chickens and dogs rise to the
heaven." They all became good soldiers of Mao when he
was deified during the sizzling movement of Red Guards.
They vowed, "to go up mountains of knives and down
to seas of flames" and "to have their bodies smashed to
powder and their bones crushed to smithereens" to fight
for and guard Mao.

But Jung and her brothers and sisters, like many other
entrapped youths, became aware that millions of people
died in famine because of the Mao's Great Leap Forward

movement. Millions of others were purged and suffered in the Cultural Revolution. They saw that many Mao's own close comrades, including his senior marshals, the national president, his hand picked successor-to-be, and their own parents, were humiliated, tortured, and persecuted. They were then bewildered and asked themselves: if the Mao's world was a paradise, what then was the hell?

As one of the best-selling non-fiction books, the *Wild Swans* is divided into 98 chapters, major portion of which portrays the Communist uprising, Mao's various political campaigns, and the exercises of his personality cult; containing the topics of Long March, Anti-Rightist Campaign, famine, Cultural Revolution, Red Guards, labor camps, etc. While recounting the stories of political chaos and social turmoil in China since the turn of the century, the author also inserts in different chapters the episodes of women status under the feudal society, traditional rituals, annual festivals, family relations and ethics, cultural conventions and taboos, and other customs, many of which have been and are still observed by the Chinese people.

The portraits of the author, her parents, and her family are included. A family tree and a chronology of family events are also provided. The author had been a red guard, a farmer, a bare-foot physician, and a factory worker. She managed to escape in 1978 to London, where she earned her doctoral degree in 1992 and began to teach at London University.

⋯⋯人要有活的信念，堅強活下去，還要有使命感，活得心安理得，無虧無欠，活得光彩四射，不要做過街老鼠，要做一個盡責尊榮的正直人，讓別人看得到你的心，讓別人知道你的愛，在心靈交會中感受到融和的快感。人本來很難理解，只要大家都能推心置腹的相待，再難的事情都能交代得明明白白，清清楚楚。

我們對別人有許多迷惑，就像別人對你有迷惑一樣。人與人相處，重在一個誠字，能誠就能破解一切的迷惑，誠是破解迷惑的一把萬能匙。

— 葉于模

HOMECARE OF ELDERLY PARENTS : A PHYSICIAN'S OWN STORY

Review of *The Final Days of My Mother,* by Kwang-ming Chen. Taichung, Taiwan: Allen Yeh, 2000.

To fulfil the oriental tradition of filial piety, Dr. Chen brought his mother to Guam to live with him and his wife, Eiko, in 1994 when she was almost 94. His mother's natural life ended in 1998 when she was 98 years old. A total of about four years, Dr. Chen performed as a special homecare physician closely attending to the needs of his mother.

As a generalist, a gerontologist, and a neurologist of his specialty, he timely appraised the physical conditions of his mother and properly treated her with whatever she needed. He and Eiko fed her, entertained her, and cleaned her day and night around the year. There were laughter and tears, delights and distresses, and satisfaction and frustration in the homecare of an advanced aged mother during the four years.

Dr. Chen presents in the work his case observation on his mother's clinical course, his personal experience as a caregiver, and his professional thoughts about homecare of elderly parents. He describes syndromes and issues of atherosclerosis, osteoporosis, and many other aging related diseases especially senile dementia; discusses treatment; and even relates to music therapy for the elderly and alternative medicine for health problems. He raises a challenging question on who cares of homecare, suggests the way of improving the quality of life, and offers the idea of applying microchip technology to human bodies.

As a personal memoir, the work also records many interesting episodes, exotic scenes, and other historical occurrences. It covers the history of Chinese exodus to Taiwan led by General Koxenga in the 1500's; the establishment of the first Presbyterian Church in Taiwan; and the story of Shoich Yokoi, a Japanese sergeant, who survived in a Talofofo cave on Guam for 28 years after World War II ended. It documents Hong Kong's returning to China, Korean Air flight 801 crash on Guam, Princess Diana and Mother Teresa's death, and Super Typhoon Parka's devastating assault on Guam.

Dr. Chen tells his own story of planting coconuts near his home at Barrigada Heights by performing incisions into the husks, like operating episiotomies for mothers with first child delivery in order to see them germinate sooner. He even alludes that he is an expertise tour guide on Guam and that he can number many Guam "ichibans" (number ones) in the world. When exhausted in running between his clinic and the hospital or totally drained with the arduous charge of homecare, Dr. Chen thought of an ancient Chinese story that he himself were the Altair boy, who met his Vega girl only once a year over the bridge across the Great River of Heaven.

When frustrated caused by his legal litigation with evil devils and lost owing to the hassle of the sophisticated politicians relating to medical concerns on Guam, he unconsciously hemmed in Japanese the poem, "A Coconut on the Beach:"

Unknown Island far away in the South Sea,
A coconut drifted to the beach where I stroll,
Thousands of miles from native land northward,
Many moons on the waves of Black Current.…

Waves after waves splashing pebbles on the sands,
Endless tides carry more coconuts from the South,
To a new home away from home,
When can it go home to their motherland?

As a prominent physician, Dr. Chen played a key role in numerous international conferences and symposia on neurological and other medical topics held in many major cities of the world. Aside from the major functions of medical congregations; he, accompanied by Eiko, also delighted his tours to many interesting sites, enjoyed fancy dining, and appreciated friendship around the world. He touches in the book classic music and those works he witnessed in Vienna, the capital of music. Back on Guam, he and Eiko once were invited as honor guests on a Japanese "mochitsuki" ceremony, making delicious mochi to cheer the New Year,

Dr. Chen edited, among others, a book entitled *Amyotrophic Lateral Sclerosis in Asia and Oceania* and published numerous significant articles in many medical journals. *The Final Days of My Mother* is another of his great works. It attaches an appendix summarizing many

aging related diseases, their diagnoses, and treatment, which alone can be a useful desk reference source. It includes bibliographical references for further reading on a variety of topics.

The book is certainly useful for practising physicians, medical students, and other medical professionals, particularly for those who are interested in gerontology, geriatrics, and homecare. It is also valuable to lay people who are interested in exploring common knowledge on medicine, details of homecare, issues of aging, etc. As a personal memoir, the work should be interesting to many academic and non-academic readers because of its catching topics in a wide range of scope. It could be, however, polished with a capable English editor and enhanced with an index.

Born in Taiwan and educated in neurology at the National Taiwan University's Medical College in Taipei, Taiwan and at the Mayo Clinic in the United States, Dr. Kwang-ming Chen was a researcher with U.S. National Institute of Neurological Diseases and Stroke on Guam during 1964-1983. He treated hundreds of Guam patients with ALS and PDC, Alzheimer's disease and other forms of senile dementia. Presently, he is an adviser to U.S. National Institute of Aging Research Center at the University of Guam.

ARE COMPUTERS SMART?

Review of *Ideas and Information: Managingin a High-Tech World* by Arno Penzias. New York: W. W. Norton, 1989. 224 pages.

In today's information age, people have experienced "abrupt collisions" with many mysterious and threatening ideas. Fiction authors have envisioned fantasies, such as "mechanical educator," which could impress on human brains, in a matter of a few minutes, knowledge and skills, which might otherwise take a lifetime to acquire. People are talking about further "human revolution," the extension or extinction of the human intellect by electronics, and even the obsolescence of men.

As Vice President of Research at AT&T Bell Laboratories and a Nobel laureate, Arno Penzias presents a different idea in his book, *Ideas and Information....* Computers are machines of unquestionable power but questionable intelligence and competence. Like telephones, microfilms, writing, arithmetic, paper, and other information technologies, computers are only another newly invented tools to help human beings transmit, store, and process information. Like other technologies, computers supplement the human mind's ability to communicate, remember, and think. Computers may perform many jobs faster and more proficient than human beings, but "the world's most powerful information tool will continue to be the human mind."

In addition to an index, the book has nine chapters dealing with information processing, words and symbols, technologies, intelligence, ideas, and the relationship between human beings and machines. As a work to demystify information processing and computer technologies, the book is written not only for computer experts but also for lay people who are in the positions of, and who are interested in, information management for making decisions.

The work contains many provoking stories. For instance, in chapter 1, it tells a story of bureaucratic mix-ups that kept the Central Park's ice-skating rink in New York City closed to the public for more than seven years before a needed repair job could be completed, accomplished not by government agencies but by the initiative of a single-minded individual. It goes on saying

that it took Ford over a billion dollars on engineering before its first Taurus rolled off a production line. The decision of the successful story relied upon the quality of information.

The difference between New York City and Ford was that New York City's mayor could not extract a viable skating rink repair proposal from his people. On the other hand, the President of Ford had a group of entrepreneurs who were able to present plans for a winning automobile. It is interesting to point out that, by comparison, the bureaucracy in the Government of Guam did better in considering that it took only fourteen steps, not seven years, for Guam teachers to obtain a box of chalk as described by Governor Joseph F. Ada.

In the same chapter, the Nobel laureate tells one of his own stories on ordering gears for a device. By the information provided, Penzias thought that the parts would have been in the mail that same afternoon when he ordered them. He was told, however, that the retail company recently purchased a computer to help it handle business, and no longer shipped orders the same day that were received before noon as the company's old catalog promised. Is it quite often that technologies would turn many business practices backward?

"Did you ask any good questions today...?" When he was asked in an interview to speculate on the reasons for his success, Isaac Isador Rabi responded with the above words from his childhood, that was his mother's usual greeting when he returned home from school each day. Rabi is another Nobel laureate, taught Penzias as a postgraduate student at Columbia, and later they met frequently at the various functions of Nobel Prize winners.

Following the discussion of this quotation, the author continues on revealing in chapter 7, "a terrible secret" of his first boss at Bell Labs, one of the smartest people in his mind. His boss felt overrated and confided:

The people around me think I'm smarter
than I really am .... They don't suspect
that I learn things more slowly than they
do and less fundamentally .... When I
listen to a presentation on something new,
the only thing that keeps me from appearing
stupid is to not ask questions about things

that others obviously already understand ....

The Nobel laureate realizes that he shares exactly the same feeling with his boss and testifies with his experience that "... we don't know what we don't know until someone asks the question."

Can you create an algorithm; devise a method for finding all the anagrams in a piece of text, such as, "Can cane sugar lead to a good deal of acne? Ex.: lead and deal. "How many barbers are there in the United States?" Why did a company recruiting an engineer ask such a question? How did the engineering graduate answer the interview question? There are numerous interesting and inspiring stories in the entire work. Check it out; you will enjoy reading it no matter you are a scholar, a student, a business manager, a computer expert, an information worker, or a layperson.

CAPTAIN AHAB: A GRIEVOUS BUT GREAT HERO

An Appreciation of *Moby Dick, or the Whale,* by Herman Melville.

Moby Dick, or the Whale, written by Herman Melville (1819-1891) in 1851, is one of the greatest American classics. It is a significant adventure story, dealing with the man's struggle against the sea and the white whale, or with the strife of human beings against the universe or the nature. The story begins with an exciting narrative; wherein Ishmael was the narrator, who presented his vision of the sea voyage and sketched his images of the knights and squires involved in the voyage.

The major figures of the story include Queequeg, Starbuck, Stubb, Tashtego, Daggoo, etc. Later in chapter XXVIII, Ahab, the protagonist of the story, stood out on the Pequod's quarterdeck. From then on, the scope of the voyage was expanded and extended; and under Ahab's command, Ishmael's sea voyage was transformed into a special expedition, designated to quest for the white

whale, or Moby Dick. After the most intolerable tension of a three-day chase, Captain Ahab was killed, the Pequod rammed, and all the crew aboard the ship except Ishmael were drowned at the end of the novel.

It is not clear what Melville had in his mind when he wrote the work. Each one of the readers will have his interpretations when he reads it. One may guess that the story told the failure and desperation of human beings; and that the nature, God or evil, was formidable and unconquerable. Others may interpret that it signified the man's battle within his own internal world or it told his conflict with the external universe.

All interpretations of the novel may have their reasonable grounds, but they may not necessarily clarify what was exactly in the author's mind. It may be these uncertainty and ambiguity that the value of the novel has kept alive all the time. The following comments and viewpoints are rendered based upon Ishmael's vision of the voyage and Melville-Ishmael's descriptions of Captain Ahab and the white whale, Moby Dick. They are also partially drawn from selected critiques on the novel.

"Call me Ishmael," the first line of the novel declared.

Except being a spectator and narrator, Ishmael, however, did not have an important role in the whole story. It seems that, in the beginning, he and his friend Queequeg were the "knights" of the sea voyage. After Ahab appeared in the scene, Ishmael and his friend were almost wholly submerged by the great waves of the high seas and by Ahab's high-lifted voice. Ishmael's status in the novel was thus attenuated

His fast bosom-friend, Queequeg, was a mystic, Yojo-worshiping harpooneer, who had "the ninetieth lay, and that's more than ever was given a harpooneer yet out of Nantucket." After signing his tattoo mark on the contract paper, he actually did not do anything significant in the whole expedition. It was in chapter CX, "nigh to his endless end," that he was put into a canoe, a coffin, which became the lifebuoy of the Pequod later. The long story of these passages could be read as a means of suspension, by which, Ahab, the protagonist, was postponed to step into the central stage.

It is natural and a necessity that Ishmael survived at the end of the story. The fact, however, did not add any weight to his role in the expedition; he was a narrator and

only a narrator of the novel. If he went down with all other crew, Moby Dick, the story, would sink to the bottom of the deep ocean, too. Who could then tell the story of the Pequod? If anyone else of the crew other than Ishmael aboard the hunting ship survived after it was shattered, Ishmael would be completely unnecessary in the novel. If Ahab were rescued, the whole story would, of course, have a different meaning.

Few readers would fail to recognize that Ishmael fell asleep in many places and his role in the story was entirely replaced by Melville himself or by other soliloquists. It is doubtful how Ishmael, a fresh sailor on the board, would know so many things about the whale. For an example, in chapter XLI, "Moby Dick" and in chapter XLII, "The Whiteness of the Whale," how he could talk about the white whale so detail before he had ever seen it.

The detailed recounting was certainly not Ishmael's but Melville's words. It is also ambiguous about who enunciated those soliloquies articulated in chapter XXIX, "Enter Ahab; to Him, Stubb" through chapter XXXI, "Queen Mab;" and in chapter XXXVI, "The Quarter-Deck" through chapter XL, "Midnight, Forecastle:" Ishmael or

Melville? The vagueness may be cleared up that the story was told by Melville- Ishmael or by the author-narrator.

It was through Ishmael that the meaning of the sea voyage, or Melville's sense in the novel, was revealed. He started at the very beginning:

.... I would sail about a little and see
the watery part of the world. It is a
way I have of driving off the spleen,
and regulating the circulation. Whenever I find myself growing grim about
the mouth; whenever it is a damp,
drizzly November in my soul; whenever
I find myself involuntarily pausing
before coffin warehouses, and bringing
up the rear of every funeral I meet;
and especially whenever my hypos get
such an upper hand of me, that it requires
a strong moral principle to prevent me
from deliberately stepping into the street,
and methodically knocking people's hats
off--then, I account it high time to get to

sea as soon as I can....

To see another part of the world other than the land and to drive off his spleen were the reasons why Ishmael wanted to go to sea.

These reasons were nothing particular; they might also be the reasons for other seamen who set out to the sea. To go to sea is a kind of life, and Ishmael's choice was only a "substitute for pistol and ball" or for others. "With a philosophical flourish, Cato throw himself upon his sword." Ishmael quietly took to the ship instead.

Ishmael's motive of going to sea was further stated in the conclusion of the first chapter:

.... the great flood-gates of the wonder-
world swung open, and in the wild conceits
that swaged me to my purpose, two and two
there floated into my inmost soul,
endless processions of the whale, and,
mid most of them all, one grand hooded
phantom, like a snow bill in the air.

It might not be his own will that Ishmael chose the sea life. He was driven or swayed to the voyage probably "by the overwhelming idea of the great whale," and by the mightiest image of the white whale. What did Ishmael find out in his sea voyage? The answer is found at the end of chapter XXXV, "The Mast-Head:"

> ... at last he loses his identity; takes
> the mystic ocean at his feet for the
> visible image of that deep, blue,
> bottomless soul, pervading mankind and
> nature; and every strange, half seen,
> gliding, beautiful thing that eludes him;
> every dimly-discovered, uprising fin of
> some undiscernible form, seems to him
> the embodiment of those elusive thoughts
> that only people the soul by continually
> flitting through it.

The watery part of the world where Ishmael set out to see was wholly fused with the wave-like forms. Ishmael was then confused and "drowned" in the mystic and

ambiguous sea.

The voyage was quite different to Captain Ahab. Who was Ahab? What a creature was he? He was first introduced in chapter XVI, "The Ship" before he actually appeared:

> .... He's a queer man, Captain Ahab—
> so some think--but a good one. Oh,
> thou'lt like him well enough; no fear,
> no fear. He's a grand, ungodly god-
> like man, Captain Ahab; doesn't speak
> much; but, when he does speak, then
> you may well listen .... Ahab's above
> the common ... he's Ahab, boy, and
> Ahab of old, thou knowest, was a
> crowned king!

Ahab was only a man, but unusual, above the common. He was not Captain Bildad, Gaptain Peleg, or any other captain; he was Ahab. Ahab was only a man, though different, yet he was not God or Satan. He was a moody good captain. He had wife and child; he had his human aspects.

Ishmael then caught first sight of Captain Ahab in chapter XXVIII, "Ahab," when the latter "stood erect, looking straight out beyond the ship's ever-pitching prow:"

There was infinity of firmest fortitude,
a determinate, unsurrenderable wilful-
ness, in the fixed and fearless, forward
dedication of that glance. Not a word he
spoke; nor did his officers say aught to
him; though by all their minutest gestures

and expressions, they plainly showed the
uneasy, if not painful, consciousness of
being under a troubled master-eye. And
not only that, but moody stricken Ahab
stood before them with a crucifixion in
his face; in all the nameless regal
overbearing dignity of some mighty woe.

Ahab was more than a man. He was a firm,
untouched, and unsurrenderable captain; a pride, solemn,
determinate and independent lord. In short, he was the
symbol of will, force, or fate.

It was such an Ahab who was seriously injured by the
white whale. He thus madly groaned in chapter XXXVI,
"The Quarter-Deck:"

... it was Moby Dick that dismasted me;
Moby Dick that brought me to this dead
stump I stand on now ... it was that accursed
white whale that razed me; made a poor
pegging lubber of me for ever and a day!

Ahab lamented in the same chapter that his suffering was not simply "from blindest instinct," and then spelled out what Moby Dick was to him:

.... All visible objects, man, are but
as paste-board masks. But in each event
--in the living act, the undoubted deed—
there, some unknown but still reasoning
thing puts forth the mouldings of its
features from behind the unreasoning mask.
If man will strike, strike through the
mask! How can the prisoner reach outside
except by thrusting through the wall?
To me, the White Whale is that wall,
shoved near to me. Sometimes I think
there's naught beyond. But 'tis enough.
He tasks me; he heaps me. I see in him
outrageous strength, with an inscrutable
malice sinewing it. That inscrutable
thing is chiefly what I hate; and be the
white whale agent, or be the white whale
principal, I will wreak that hate upon

him. Talk not to me of blasphemy, man;
I'd strike the sun if it insulted me.
For could the sun do that, then could I
do the other....

In Ahab's mind, the visible object of Moby Dick
stood for a pasteboard mark, a prison wall, wherein
harbored outrageous strength sinewing with an inscrutable
malice. Being a prisoner, he determined to strike through
the mask, the wall.

In chapter XLI, "Moby Dick," the white whale was
further portrayed as seen by Melville:

.... The White Whale swam before him as
the monomaniac incarnation of all those
malicious agencies which some deep men
feel eating in them, till they are left
living on with half a heart and half a
lung. That intangible malignity which
has been from the beginning; to whose
dominion even the modern Christians
ascribe one-half of the worlds; which

the ancient Ophites of the east
reverenced in their statue devil;--
Ahab did not fall down and worship it
like them; but deliriously transferring
its idea to the abhorred white whale, he
pitted himself, all mutilated, against it....

It was those "deep" men, of them Captain Ahab was a representative, who felt the white whale eating in them: it was not those "shallows," like Starbuck, Captain Gardiner, or any other captain, who would have such a feeling. The "shallows" sailed only for fishes, worked only "by mouth, or by the job, or by the profit." And the intangible malignity of the white whale was from the beginning.

Hence, in the same chapter, Ahab "piled upon the whale's white hump the sum of all the general rage and hate felt by his whole race from Adam down; and then, as if his chest had been a mortar, he burst his hot heart's shell upon it." The general rage and hate was not only Ahab's, but was felt by his whole race from Adam down. So, in chapter XXXVI, Ahab, the representative of his race, shouted out his determined will:

.... I'll chase him （Moby Dick） round
Good Hope, and round the Horn, and
round the Norway Maelstrom, and round
perdition's flames before I give him
up. And this is what ye have shipped
for, men! to chase that white whale
on both sides of land, and over all
sides of earth, till he spouts black
blood and rolls fin out....

But Moby Dick was unconquerable; he would never
spout black blood and roll fin out. Note in chapter XLI:

... although other leviathans might be
hopefully pursued, yet to chase and point
lances at such an apparition as the Sperm
Whale was not for mortal man. That to
attempt it, would be inevitably to be
torn into a quick eternity....

.... Moby Dick was ubiquitous; that he

had actually been encountered in opposite
latitudes at one and the same instant of
time....

... after repeated, intrepid assaults,
the White Whale had escaped alive....
Moby Dick not only ubiquitous but
immortal ... though groves of spears
should be planted in his flanks, he
would still swim away unharmed....

In short, Moby Dick was ubiquitous and immortal; he
could not be harmed and conquered by a mortal man.

The white of the white whale in chapter XLII,
"The Whiteness of the Whale," can be conceived as two
different connotations. The white in the forms of the polar
bear, the albatross, the Albino man, the corpse, the shroud,
and the ghost would evoke sinister and terror to the man's
soul. While it is in the forms of the bridal veil, the white
hairs of the old, the ermine of the judge, and the alb of the
Christian priest, it would be perceived as benignity and
gentleness to the human mind. Moby Dick, as the nature,

then could be looked upon as a neutral symbol, that could be either wicked or virtuous, or neither harmful nor helpful to the world.

What Moby Dick might really be and actually stand for has been briefly explored. Why, then, would Captain Ahab, a mortal man, have the motive to chase Moby Dick, the immortal white whale? Ahab answered the question in chapter CXXXII, "The Symphony:"

> What is it, what nameless, inscrutable,
> unearthly thing is it; what cozening,
> hidden lord and master, and cruel,
> remorseless emperor commands me; that
> against all natural lovings and longings,
> I so keep pushing, and crowding, and
> jamming myself on all the time;
> recklessly making me ready to do what
> in my own proper, natural heart, I
> durst not so much as dare? Is Ahab,
> Ahab? Is it I, God, or who, that
> lifts this arm? But if the great sun
> move not of himself; but is as an

errand-boy in heaven; nor one
single star can revolve, but by some
invisible power; how then can this
one small heart beat; this one small
brain think thoughts; unless God does
that beating, does that thinking,
does that living, and not I. By
heaven, man, we are turned round and
round in this world like yonder
windlass, and Fate is the handspike ....

Although Ahab was determined to chase the white
whale, he had been a moody captain before he saw "there
she blows." During the three-day chase, he was quite
aware that he might be desperate. "The sound of hammers,
and the hum of the grindstone was heard...." "I feel now
like a billow that's all one crested comb.... I am old;
--shake hands with me, man." Often looming in his mind
was: "Is my journey's end coming?"

Nevertheless, Ahab stood out as a missionary in
chapter CXXXIV, "The Chase--Second Day,": "....
Ahab is forever Ahab, man. This whole act's immutably

decreed. 'Twas rehearsed by thee and me a billion years before this ocean rolled. Fool! I am the Fate's lieutenant; I act under orders...." It was God, not Ahab, who lifted his arm to chase the white whale. Ahab was only an involuntary volunteer, only a hero on the round windlass. His whole act was "immutably decreed;" his order was "under orders."

He obeyed God, but disobeyed, or denied, himself. It was a hard strife between the obeying and the disobeying, as "The Sermon" preached by Father Mapple in Chapter IX,

> ... all things that God would have us do
> are hard for us to do.... He oftener
> commands us than endeavors to persuade.
> And if we obey God, we must disobey
> ourselves; and, it is in this disobeying
> ourselves, wherein the hardness of
> obeying God consists.

The novel as a whole may reveal that Melville was not agreeable with Emerson's transcendentalism. The latter considered all-is-good and "all-is-well" in the world. For Emerson, nature is beautiful and benevolent to man. The work may also spell out that the author carried a different idea on the "sweetness and light" of the romantic writers in his era.

Melville probably was also attempting to paint in the novel the Plato's idea of dichotomous worlds: one material and the other, spiritual. All the crewmen, except Captain Ahab, aboard the Pequod were living in an everyday material planet. As "shallows," not one of them could comprehend Ahab, a "deep" and "spiritual" man, who was hovering in a different level of universe. The white whale in the picture could be a Plato's symbol, which "can be ugly and beautiful, good and bad, just and unjust...."

As narrated in the work, men were enslaved and dominated by the white whale "from the beginning" and "from Adam down." Men, as Ahab put it, lived in the world only like the prisoners of the white whale; "to whose dominion even the modern Christians ascribe one-half of the worlds; which the ancient Ophites of the east reverenced in their statue." But Captain Ahab, the deep, spiritual man, did not fall down and worship it. He comprehended the

invisible thing behind the visible pasteboard mark, and claimed that the only way the prisoners could reach outside was to break through the wall between the visible and the invisible.

Although Moby Dick, the wall, was ubiquitous and immortal, although Ahad was quite pessimistic in his quest to strike through the wall, he was never discouraged and never gave up. "Ahab is for ever Ahab!" He held fast the fundamental doctrine: God dominates; men do their best. Under God's order, Ahab had indeed done what he could have done. Even at the end when Moby Dick's "glittering mouth yawned beneath the boat like an open-doored marble tomb," he still "seized the long bone（Moby Dick's tooth）with his naked hands, and wildly strove to wrench it from its gripe." At last, "he was shot out of the boat, ere the crew knew he was gone." Yes, he was killed, but he was not defeated, and his voyage's end was much better than Ishmael's. Ishmael, though survived, was actually "drowned."

All men were destined to die. The only difference was that "some men die at ebb tide; some at low water; some at the full of the flood." Ahab fully realized the reality of life. To him, death was just like the fact as Queequeg lying in the canoe, a coffin, which was a real lifebuoy for a man. As a whole, the novel may be read as a revelation of the effort, courage, and fortitude of man in his struggle with the world, nature, or Moby Dick, the white whale. Like Homer's Achilles, Melville's Ahab in the struggle was indeed the most grievous, but the greatest "ungodly godlike" hero. It was Ahab himself that proclaimed: "I feel my topmost greatness lies in my topmost grief."

Selected Readings:

Cunliffe, Marcus. *The Literature of the United States.* Baltimore, MD: Penguin Books, 1967. 3d ed.

Feidelson, Charles. *Symbolism and American Literature.* Chicago: University of Chicago Press, 1953.

Gardiner, Harold C. *American Classics Reconsidered: a Christian Appraisal.* New York: Scribner, 1958.

Melville, Herman. *Moby Dick, or the Whale.* Garden City, NY: Garden City Publishing, 1937.

Plato. *Plato's The Republic.* New York: Random House, 196?.

Stewart, Randall. *American Literature and Christian Doctrine.* Baton Rouge, LA: Louisiana State University Press, 1958.

Thorp, Willard. *Herman Melville: Representative Selections with Introduction, Bibliography, and Notes.* New York: American Book, 1938.

A BRIEF SUMMARY OF
OLD GOLD MOUNTAIN

by Lisa See. New York: St. Martin, 1995. 394 p.

Summary:

The work tells the story of the author's great-grand father, Fong See, in the Gold Mountain: how he emigrated from a Chinese village in Kwangtung to the United States, how he married a Caucasian woman, Lettice Pruetty, and how he became one of the most prominent Chinese in the United States.

Excerpts of the Story:

Wilbur Woo ... was one of the fifteen Chinese students at UCLA. After the War （WWII）, some of us became professionals--doctors, lawyers.... But things hadn't really improved. I remember driving to Sacramento in the late forties and being stopped by a policeman. The first thing he asked was "what restaurant do you work at?" Choey Lau, Fong Yun's eldest daughter, married an

army air force pilot who couldn't get a civilian job because he was a Chinese. In 1951, they would move to Hawaii, where he would be hired by Aloha Airline, which had been found by a Chinese.

In New York, when the chief Chinese delegate to the United Nations knocked on the door of the wrong hotel room, the women who answered wordlessly handed him her laundry. James Wong Howe, a cinematographer, took a portion of his Hollywood money to open a Chinese restaurant. When a photographer came to take publicity shots of the exterior, Howe walked over and asked, "can you move over just a little bit so it will make a better composition?" The photographer sneered. "What the hell do you know about photography? Why don't you go back in the kitchen and do some cooking?"

The boys（Fong See's grants and their relatives and friends）... were like so much hollow bamboo, Chinese on the outside, hollow on the inside. They did not fit into the world of their parents. They certainly didn't fit into the world of their white peers. They didn't even fit in with girls in Chinatown. The basic philosophies did not mesh. The American work ethic--success, occupational prestige

... just didn't jibe with how these boys had been raised: to save for buying trips and banquets, to work for the family and to yourself, to think of returning home to China, and not to disgrace yourself in front of Americans or bring harm to the family through your actions.

Like their fathers and grandfathers before them, who had suffered from having their culture belittled, so too did these young men. The larger world spoke loudly and clearly. You are different. What you feel has no value. You are bad, you are dirty, you are unpleasant to live near ....

.... and sometimes the younger kids pumped the pedals, creating horrible wheezing moans. Even without the organ, the noise level was always high. Nine people lived in this apartment: Richard's grandfather, his wife, and their seven children, ranging in age from infancy to their early twenties. They were often joined by what seemed like half the population of Chinatown, who came over unannounced to sit and gape before the new television set--the first in the neighborhood. Over the cacophony of voices--babies crying, teenagers giggling and roughhousing, old folks calling out to each other

in high-pitched tones--the set blare out wrestling or newscasts.

Richard didn't pay much attention to his grandfather or Ngon Hung. His grandfather seemed fossilized. His step-grandmother--though just a couple of years older than his aunt Sissee--appeared ancient, with her crooked back and her shuffling steps. Carrying, birthing, and caring for seven babies had taken a toll. Following ghetto tradition, all of her children had been born at home--some easily, as when she went to the bathroom and the baby simply slipped out, and some--according to family story--with difficulty, as when she was home alone, in pain, and pushing for hours.

AN INTRODUCTION TO
THE TALE OF GENJI

by Murasaki Shikibu. New York: Alfred A. Knopf, 1977.

Introduction:

The Tale of Genji is a long romance, 54 chapters, describing the court life of Heian Japan from the 10th century into the 11th. It is probably the work of a single hand, that of a court lady known as Murasaki Shikibu, with possible accretions during the two following centuries.

Murasaki may derive either from the name of an important lady in the Genji itself or from the fact that it means purple. Fuji, the first half of her family name, means wisteria 紫籐. She came from a cadet branch of the great Fujiwara family, which ruled the land through most of the Heian period. She was married in 998 or 999 and died in 1015. She went to court in the service of Empress Akiko or Shoshi sometime around the middle of the first decade of the 11th century.

The actions of the Genji cover almost three generations of a century. The first 41 chapters have to do with the life and loves of a nobleman known as shining Genji. The hero of the last ten chapters, Kaoru, who posses in the world as Genji's son but is really the grandson of his best friend, is five at the time of Genji's last appearance and 28 in the last chapter. One of the things the Genji means that the good days are in the past.

The tale may break into three parts. The first part has a great deal of the tenth century in it. The hero is an idealized prince, whose early career is a success story. After the three transitional chapters came what are generally called the Uji chapters. The pessimism grows; the main action moves from the capital to the village of Uji, both character and action are more attenuated 減色. Many have argued that the Uji chapters are by someone else. Tradition has assigned the authorship of these chapters to Shikibu's daughter, Daini no Sammi. Changes and additions may have come later, but the narrative points essentially to a single author working over a long period of time.

Excerpts of Few Sample Paragraphs:

In the Paulownia Court, Genji or Minamota, was born. He was named as such as a commoner. His mother was one of the most favored ladies in the court. She died not long after Genji was born due to jealousy and pressure infringing upon her in the court. Genji soon became the shining one. He was also favored by his father, the emperor .... "It is the face of one who should ascend to the highest place and be father to the nation."

That nose (homophonous with flower) now dominated the scene. It was like that of the beast on which Samantabhadra rides, long, pendulous, and red. A frightful

nose. The skin was whiter than snow, a touch bluish（depressed, dispirited）even. The forehead bulged and the line over the cheeks suggested that the full face would be very long indeed. She was pitifully thin. He could see through her robes how narrow her shoulders were. ... the visage was such an extraordinary one that he could not immediately take his eyes away. The shape of the head and the flow of the hair were very good, little inferior, he thought, to those of ladies whom he had held to be great beauties. The hair fanned out over the hem of her robes with perhaps a foot to spare.... Over a sadly faded singlet she wore a robe discolored with age to a murky drab and a rather splendid sable 黑貂皮 jacket, richly perfumed, such as a stylish lady might have worn a generation or two before. It was entirely wrong for a young princess, but he feared that she needed it to keep off the winter cold. He was as mute as she had always been; but presently he recovered sufficiently to have yet another tries at shaking her from her muteness. He spoke of this and that, and the gesture as she raised a sleeve to her mouth was somehow stiff and antiquated. He thought of a master of court rituals taking up his position akimbo 兩手乂腰. She managed a smile for him, which did not seem to go with the rest of her. It was too awful. He hurried to get his things together.

One could not be angry with her. Commonness and honest, sturdy indignation could be charming. The trouble was with her speech. She had grown up among country people, and it was very inelegant. Pure, precise speech can give a certain distinction to rather ordinary remarks. An impromptu 即席的 poem, for instance, if it is spoken musically, with an air at the beginning and end as of something unsaid, can seem to convey words of meaning, even if upon mature reflection it does not seem to have said much of anything at all. Torrential remarks have the opposite effect: the distinguished seems flat and vulgar. The overemphatic Omi speech patterns made everything seem less than serious. She had acquired them at her nurse's breast and was not shy about using them; and they were all wrong. Yet she did have her little accomplishments. She could without warning rattle off poem after poem of approximately the right length, and if the top half did not seem to go with the bottom half, that was all right too.

Women were visible in the dim light beyond. Two or three had come forward and were leaning against the balustrades 欄干. Who might they be? Though in casual dress, they managed to look very elegant in multicolored robes that blended pleasantly in the twilight. Akikonomu had sent some little girls to lay out insect cages in the damp garden. They had on robes of lavender and pink and various deeper shades of purple and yellow-green jackets lined with green, all appropriately autumnal hues. Disappearing and reappearing among the mists, they made a charming picture. Four and five of them with cages of several colors were walking among the wasted flowers; picking a wild carnation here and another flower there for their royal lady. The wind seemed to bring a scent from even the scentless asters 紫花, most delightfully, as if Akikonomu's own sleeves had brushed them.

簡介伏琥著《清宮秘聞》

— 香港海峰出版社，一九九六年

　　以短篇方式，分別摘錄從努爾哈赤、皇太極，到宣統清朝三百年間宮庭中的異聞趣事，但非正史。題目有滿族起源神話、康熙與聊齋、香妃之死、丐王宴、女爸爸、李蓮英、光緒之死等。中國之所以不進步，為西方列強欺凌，完全由於清皇室的昏庸，沒有科學知識，不懂世界事務；尤其慈禧，一個無知無識的女人，憑著一點小聰明，玩弄權術，蠻橫殘暴地統治中國四十年，兒皇帝只是她的傀儡，為她所用，虐待，甚至殺害。

　　軼聞雖非正史，但不外二種來源：一是皇室御用文人，製造出來，歌頌天子；另外則是傳聞於鄉野，對殘暴統治，不能直接表達意見，而以故事傳述，譏諷皇朝，廣為流傳，後者可以看到民聲反應。無論如何，為政者所作所為，關係民生，關係國家興衰，這樣的書，對他們應有警告和警惕的作用。

《冰點》抄摘

簡介：

　　《冰點》，三浦綾子作，林靜文譯，台北小暢書房印行，一九九八年，三三一頁。主要人物：辻口啟造，醫生、醫院院長；夏枝，醫生太太；陽子，醫生收養的女兒；背景：一九四六年日本戰敗以後，發生於作者的家鄉北海道。主題： 愛你的敵人，反復爭扎，啟造始終都沒有做到。

摘要：

　　《冰點》一書，以作者三浦綾子的家鄉北海道冰天雪地為背景，展開人類原罪的探討。醫生啟造，擁有一家醫院，工作忙碌。為了美麗的妻子夏枝頸項印有村井靖夫的吻痕，長年懷疑她與村井之間不尋常的關係，忌恨在心。因此收養了殺死他小女兒麗子的兇手的女兒陽子，作為報復妻子的不貞。進而陷害夏枝，並帶給自己無限深痛。

摘錄：

　　陽子不記仇恨，善良純潔，一心一意為他人著想，這正是神的形像。陽子最後自殺，像徵了基督對苦難心靈的救贖。她犧牲自己的生命，喚醒千千萬萬迷途的羔羊，表現了悲天憫人的心懷。

敵人就是非跟他和好不可的人。

世界上再也沒有比耶穌所說的「愛你的敵人」這句話更難學的了。一般的只要努力，就能夠完成，但愛自己的敵人，卻不是努力就能夠辦得到的。

夏枝覺得，現在正應了天遣的話。對丈夫以外的男人傾心時，責罰便立刻下來，這不是天遣嗎？

「爸爸的手好大」（麗子所說）。辻口啟造一直疑視著自己的手，這雙手挽救不了麗子的生命，徒有一雙大手，卻沒有一點用途。

對佐石土雄（殺死麗子的兇手，陽子的生父）而言，可能也是不幸，如果沒有碰到麗子，他也就不會殺人了。這一想，偶然的可怕，使啟造不寒而慄。

那是對朋友說的話，辻口先生說愛你的敵人時，是他沒有敵人的時侯。雖然外表是正人君子，正人君子大部份都屬於怪物。

其實，醫學博士辻口啟造，和殺人兇手佐石土雄，都是同一類的人。

自從失去了麗子後，夏子才瞭解，每天平安無事的度過，比甚麼都重要。

人對於自己的過失，總是容易遺忘。

才想到這事。想到自己的孩子被殺死，已夠悲慘了，還要終生懷著仇恨 — 無法發洩的仇恨，豈不太傻。我不想一輩子活在這種痛苦中。要避免這樣，唯有不懷恨兇手。要怎樣才不恨他？那麼，只有表示愛。

我現在只剩下兩條路可走，就是終生懷恨兇手，或努力實現「愛你的敵人」這句話。懷著仇恨，生活是悲哀的，我寧可愛那孩子（陽子）。

沒有能力的孩子要鼓勵他，貧窮人家的孩子，往往比富家子弟更具獨立…對軟弱的孩子，要格外和氣…。

不論那種人，都不要拒絕，重視每個人…古代聖人說過，不重視人，就是罪惡的根源。有各種各樣孩子就讀的學校有甚麼不好？大學也是一樣，愈是所謂名門，優越感愈強，結果只有愈瞧不起人而已。

你喜歡這個人，這個人不一定是好人。反過來說，你以為討厭這人，但這人並不一定是壞人。

很久以前，我丟了十塊錢，撿到的人，一定很高興。我很高興撿到的人高興，如果是乞丐撿去，就更好啦。

丟了十塊錢，是因為十塊錢遺失了，當然是損失。如果你再念念不忘地想著損失、損失，那損失就更大啦。

丟了一百塊錢，應該有一百塊錢的快樂。只要想，幸好沒有丟了兩百塊錢，那就不會悶悶不樂了；或者也可以想，那撿到錢的人，已經餓得快要死了，幸好撿到這一百塊錢，救回了生命，這不是很好嗎？如果念念不忘那一百塊錢，那才是大損失。

鏡中照出眼睛看得見的東西，照不出眼睛看不見的東西。

面對著死神的人，一切地位、醫術都徒然失效。站在死亡邊緣的啟造，沒有任何心理準備。他身為醫生，目睹過多少的死，然而死的都是他人，而非他自己。現在啟造對自己的命運，束手無策。

…啟造輕輕捉住雪蟲，但牠立刻死了，如若一片雪，被手指一觸就溶化，脆弱可憐。

所謂幸福、和平，就是像這些雪蟲。自從這次死裡逃生，啟造瞭解了生命是具有多麼嚴肅的意義。

活著是與在大浪中奮鬥具有相同的意義吧？啟造祈求著和平、愉快的生活，浪濤卻不斷對他捲過來。

愛就是像他那樣，把自己的生命奉獻給對方。

我知道「愛你的敵人」這句話，但只貼著標語，不能算是愛人。那位神父一定瞭解更重要的意義，瞭解不是詞彙所表示，而是更深刻真諦。

到孤兒院來物色孩子的傢伙，我最不順眼的就是這個，好像孤兒院的孩子低人一等似的。甚麼苦工的孩子，勞動者的孩子，跟我們的孩子，有多大的差別？

每次有人到孤兒院參觀時，看到他們一個個都扮著一付像是高人的面孔，我總是忍不住的想，我和這些孤兒究竟有甚麼不同？

你們家好像家世淵博，但真正說起來，人都是殺人兇手。有的人娶姨太太，使太太受苦；有的人參加戰爭殺人，沒有一個家庭的祖先之中，沒有這樣的人吧？

要做到真真疼愛陽子，單單看聖經有甚麼用？聖經上的字，走馬看花似地經過啟造的眼睛，卻不進入他的心，他仍沒有真誠的信仰。

在希望你哭的人面前哭，就是你輸了。這時候如果能夠笑一笑，那麼，我想你就會精神百倍。

雲層上面有光明的太陽。我們遇到困難時，總是害怕、慌張、不知所措。但如果知道那只是一層薄雲，穿越之後，光明的太陽就重新照射，那麼，就鎮靜地採取行動吧。

我只看到半邊的天。是的，不論甚麼事，我都只看到一半。

不願意把自己的過失，歸咎於別人。自己變壞，應該由自己負責⋯⋯我不是溪流，我是人，即使我被撥了髒水，我仍然不要失去本來的面目。

死，能解決問題嗎？對已經自殺而死的人，他所說的個人存在價值問題，決不因此而解決。社會愈複雜，個人的人格價值愈被忽視，於是，人的存在範圍便不得不縮小。也許死不是解決、而是提出問題，尤其自殺，更是這樣。

以生命為賭注，而提出問題，其周圍的人和社會，能夠給予這個問題解答的，恐怕很少。

啟造回顧自己走過的人生路程，覺得毫無意義，他不知道自己為甚麼活著？

人活著總有個目標吧。我在社會上有地位，有一小筆財產，也有美貌的妻子，但這些並未使我幸福。

在他人眼中，這是個幸福美滿的模範家庭，事實上有點不可思議。也許每個家庭都有丈夫拈花惹草，妻子紅杏出牆，婆媳不和，兒女不成器等羞於告人的家醜。但人人都知道家醜不可外揚，表面上都維護著體面。這些被隱瞞的家醜，由於某種動機，而演變成自殺、出走、殺人、離婚等時，才為社會所知。

如果我偶然逢場作戲，我決不會責備自己。然而，我卻不能原諒妻子的出軌，這是甚麼道理。別人所做的壞事，由我來做，也不一定是壞事。

　　一個拿出全身力氣在跑路的人，即使絆著一個小石頭，也會爬不起來。

　　我絕對不因為對我有惡意的人而改變我的性格，那是愚蠢的。要我苦惱，要我悲哀，我決不苦惱，決不悲哀。

　　即使我不是殺人兇手的女兒，我的父親，或他的親戚，母親或她的親戚，總有一兩位是做過壞事的人。

　　在每一個社會體制內，基督教義是潛移默化的酵素，不是消滅異類的嘔吐劑。

　　　　　　　　　　　　　　　　　── George H. Dunne

　　一般的慈善工作，給的是「身外」之物，給後只讓自己覺得更高高在上。奉獻則是把「自己」的一部份獻出來，是去做窮苦人的僕人，來服侍他們，作後的感覺則是謙卑、不足。

　　奉獻最初目的不是為了「自己」，而是為了「別人」呀！奉獻的最原始動機，應該是「愛」，愛那需要妳扶一把的小弟兄！

　　不論那一種奉獻，若只為自己，自我犧牲便成了為自己加冕、立碑的一個手段，那是自私。

　　高站在卡車上往下丟（救濟品）的人，永遠比在下面擠著接的人有福。

　　貧窮、病痛與飢餓的人，需要的不只是金錢、健康、與食物，他們就像所有的人一樣，需要的是一種生存意義 —— 一種次序感，歸屬感，與一個活下去的理由。當一些有心人在幫助窮苦人找工作，找安身之處時，若能為他找到生存的意義時，才是真正在他的生命深處，幫助了他。

　　人與人的生命是連在一起的，每個人的苦難，都與自己息息相關，都應提醒我們身為人的目的。唯有走出自己的家門，走進對方的生活裡，把「自己」的一部分給出去，參進別人的生命裡，然後生命才能真正影響生命。如此，你造福了別人，同時，也更豐富了自己。

—— 陳惠琬

淺識中國舊體詩

—《全英譯魯迅舊體詩》札記

Von Kowallis, Jon Eugene. *The Lyrical Lu Xun:*
A Study of His Classical-Style Verse. Honolulu,
HI: University of Hawaii Press, 1996. 378 p.

七言絕句 heptasyllabic quatrain：

四行，每行七字。見下例：

別諸弟三首 之二　一九〇〇年三月

　　還家未久又離家，日暮新愁分外加；
　　夾道萬株楊柳樹，望中都化斷腸花。

Parting from My Brothers 2 of 3

　　Returned home but a while,
　　　　again I'm leaving home;
　　And now the dusk adds extra bite
　　　　to sadness where I roam.
　　Ten thousand willows line the road

on which I have departed

Gazing deep therein, I see them change

to flowers brokenhearted.

The form of versification employed here is heptasyllabic or "seven-character" quatrain. A related form is the pentasyllabic quatrain（see below）, which has also been called a "five-character quatrain. The seven-character quatrain has four lines, each seven characters in length, whereas the five-character quatrain has four lines of but five characters each. These quatrain 絕句 forms are akin to a regulated verse 律詩 in that they must adhere to the same strict rhyme schemes and tone patterns, but they differ from the 律詩 in that they have four lines instead of eight and not follow the same strictures as regards the use of antithetical couplets.

五言絕句 pentasyllabic quatrain:

四行，每行五字。見下例：

庚子送灶即事　一九〇一年

隻雞膠牙糖，典衣供瓣香；

家中無長物，豈獨少黃羊。

Seeing Off the Kitchen God in the Year of 1901

A chicken and the "teeth-gluing sweet,"
Clothing pawned for incense that we mete.
Our household, of every last thing depleted,
Still more than a yellow lamb has been deleted!

七言律詩 heptasyllabic regulated verse:

八行，每行七字，一、二、四、六、八行押韻，
第一行的韻可以省去。中間四行，形成兩對對仗句
two antithetical couplets。見下例：

蓮篷人　一九○○年八月

蔟裳荇帶處仙鄉，風定猶聞碧玉香；
鷺影不來秋瑟瑟，葦花伴宿露瀼瀼；
掃除膩粉呈風骨，褪卻紅衣學淡妝；
好向濂溪稱淨植，莫隨殘葉墮寒塘。

Lotus Seedpod People

In water-caltrop raiment clad, with belt of
　　floating-heart, you dwell in faerie wonderlands.
Such lush jade-green, your perfumed hue—
　　tho' wind may cease, its fragrance yet expands.

Egrets' reflections grace this pond no more,

    only the autumn wind's soughing,

      a soughing so glum.

Alone, but for the rush flower, you bear the nocturne,

    wake and await the heavy dew that with

    the morn will come.

With greasy makeup swept away,

    true character takes form!

Red garments loud, stripped off display

    strength of a subtler norm!

Live up to what Lianxi said:

    stand up "so straight and tall."

Follow not the withered leaves

    in chilly ponds to fall!

The type of versification employed in this poem is 七言律詩 heptasyllabic regulated verse, sometimes referred to as "seven-character regulated verse" because it has eight lines, seven characters in length. There is a related style called 五言律詩 pentasyllabic regulated verses（see below）：eight lines of but five characters in length. Both the seven-character and five-character regulated verse styles have strict rhyme schemes and fixed tonal patterns. In a seven-character regulated verse style such as Lu Xun employs in this poem on 蓮篷人, rhyme occurs at the end of the first, second, fourth, sixth, and eighth lines （that at the end of the first line may be omitted）. In a five-character regulated verse, rhyme also falls at the end of the second, fourth, sixth, and eighth lines; rhyme at the end of the first line also being optional.

　　五言律詩 pentasyllabic regulated verse。八行，每行五字，二、四、六、八行押韻，首行的韻亦可省略，中間四行必須形成兩對對仗句。見下例：

哀范君（范愛農）　一九一二年七月

　　風雨飄搖日，余懷范愛農；
　　華顛萎寥落，白眼看雞蟲；
　　世味秋茶苦，人間直道窮；
　　奈何三月別，竟爾失畸躬。

Mourning Fan Ainong 1 of 3

　　Mid whirling wind and rain this day,
　　My memories of Ainong stay.
　　With thinning, dry, and graying hair
　　How his eyes would roll at the scrappers for fare!

His gorge rose at men's worldly lust—

What gain's in store for those who're just?

Three months away, at such a cost—

This uncouth friend I've truly lost.

絕句 quatrain 與律詩 regulated verse 相似，兩者均有嚴格韻律和聲律的規範。只是絕句為四行，不必使用嚴格的對仗。

The rhyme category of a given Chinese character in classical verse is dictated by its antiquated reading rather than its pronunciation in modern Mandarin. For the purpose of tone patterns in such classical verse, words in Chinese were classified as belonging to either the 平聲 level tone or the 仄聲 deflected tone, even though there are four different tones in modern Mandarin, and even more existed in the spoken Chinese of the early Tang dynasty when "regulated verse" became an established form.

As might well be imagined, much memorization and practice was necessary to become adept at these verse forms. They confine the poetry in terms of length, rhyme, and tone patterns, as well as requiring that a poem's middle four lines form two antithetical couplets. But the

attraction of these forms by lay in their ability to furnish educated persons with an almost irresistible challenge to show literary prowess and verbal acumen in the pithy, metaphor-laden medium that became classical Chinese verse.

Although in 古詩，characters in the eleventh and thirteenth rhyming categories are considered interchangeable, in 律詩 and 絕句，this is hardly ever the case. Lu Xun's verse is intended as a 五言律詩，so he has stretched the rules a bit here, employing neighboring rhyme. This was frequently done at the time and does not detract from the artistic quality of these verse.

奇體五言律詩

贈鄔其山 Uchiyama Kanzo（作者日本友人）。
一九三一年

廿年居上海，每日見中華；
有病不求藥，無聊纔讀書；
一闊臉就變，所砍頭漸多；
忽而又下野，南無阿彌陀。

For Wu Qishan (Uchiyama Kanzo), March 1931

Twenty years in Shanghai did you stay,
Glimpsing China's splendors every day:
Afflictions for which medicine's not sought,
And study just as boredom's afterthought;
A volte-face when fortune comes their way?—
Decapitations increase by the day.
Then suddenly they're on the outs again,
Let's trust the Amitabha Lord, Amen!

Though the poem is at first glance written in the style of 五言律詩，it fails to conform to the strict rhyme scheme set down traditionally for that verse form. Aside from a slight incongruity in the first line, the word 華 at the end of the second line falls into the tonal classification of 下平聲 lower level-tone and belongs to the rhyme category of 麻。 The word 書 at the end of the fourth line is a 上平聲 upper level-tone in the rhyme category of 魚。 The sixth line ends with the character 多，which falls under the rhyme category of 歌。 The poet then has the last line end with 陀。 That character is, like 多，in the category of 歌。

In view of the above, the poet has employed three separate rhymes and has overstepped the bounds for complying with the strict rules of the regulated verse form. Judging from the depth of Lu Xun's knowledge of classical Chinese poetics, it is not likely that he would make an error. There are two possible explanations for the form employed: one, that this was deliberately intended as a style of 打油詩 doggerel verse to emphasize farcical overtones; the second has been suggested by Lu Xun's old friend 許壽裳: ""贈鄔其山"中，the use of 華、魚、多、陀 in the same rhyme is in accordance with the conventions of the 古詩 style. But this use of characters from the 麻 and 魚 categories as rhyming words in a poem of regulated-verse style may indeed be termed unconventional 奇特。"

百年中國文學的背景是一片蒼茫的灰色，在灰色雲層空茫處，殘留著上一個世紀末慘烈的晚照。那是一八四〇年虎門焚煙的餘燼，那是一八六〇年火燒圓明園的殘焰，那是一八九四年黃海海戰北洋艦隊沉船前最後一道光痕⋯⋯

——謝冕

文學的理由

高行健接受二〇〇〇年諾貝爾文學獎講稿語錄

　　一個人不可能成為神，更別說替代上帝。由超人來主宰這個世界，祇能把這世界攪得更亂，更加糟糕。

　　文學一旦弄成國家的頌歌，民族的旗幟，政黨的喉舌，或階級與集團的代言，儘管可以動用傳播手段，聲勢浩大，鋪天蓋地而來；這樣的文學，也就喪失天性，不成為文學，而變成權力和利益的代用品。

　　冷的文學，是一種逃亡、而求生存的文學，是一種不讓社會扼殺，而求得精神上自救的文學；一個民族倘寬容不下這樣一種非功利的文學，不僅是作家的不幸，也該是這個民族的悲哀。

　　文學並不旨在顛覆，而貴在發現和揭示鮮為人知或知之不多，或以為知道、其實不甚了了的人世的真相。真實是文學顛撲不破的最基本品格。

　　文學不只是對現實的視寫，它切入現實的表層，深深觸及到現實的底蘊；它揭開假象，又高高凌駕於日常的表象之上，以宏觀的視野，來顯示事態的來龍去脈。

　　文學也訴諸想像，然而，這種精神之旅，並非胡說八道；脫離真實感受的想像，離開生活經驗的根據去虛構，只能落得蒼白無力……誠然，文學並非只訴諸日常生活的經驗，作家也不囿於親身的經歷；耳聞目睹、以及在別人的文學作品中已經陳述過的，通過語言的載體，也能成為自己的感受，這也是文學語言的魅力。

　　人類的歷史，如果只由那不可知的規律左右，盲目的潮流來來去去，而聽不到個人異樣的聲音，不免令人悲哀。從這個意義上說，文學正是對歷史的補充。

雋 永 集

請求翻譯 胡獻群講，周勻之轉述

四川人能說善道，會擺龍門，一位四川朋友請客，問第一位客人怎樣來的，客人說是走路來的，主人說，你真自在。第二位是坐轎子來的，主人說，你好安逸。第三位是騎馬來的，主人說，你好威風。第四位是坐車來的，主人說，你好快當。第五位故意說是爬來的，主人說，你真踏實。第六位說是滾來的，主人說，老兄真周到。── 請譯英文。

黎元洪是基督 陳若融口述

月前，有數批中國同胞，偷渡來了關島，被送到了移民局，經過詢問，每人理由充足，要求政治庇護。甲編六四，乙說墮胎。某君則說，他信基督，參加家庭教會，受到迫害。

移民官：「基督叫甚麼名字？」

偷渡客：「黎元洪。」

移民官：「他怎麼死的？」

偷渡客：「被槍斃的。」

法庭嚴肅，移民官裝模作樣，抽了抽褲帶。

屁頌　　　　　清「遊戲主人」編《笑林廣記》

前清一秀才，死後見了閻王，適逢閻王放了一屁，作起了屁頌：　伏維大王，高聳金臀，洪宣寶屁；依稀乎絲竹之聲，彷彿乎麝蘭之氣；臣立下風，不勝馨香之味。

話屁　　　　　孫如陵

明末，有陳因者，善說笑話，一日，因酒誤闖禁地，為太監拘禁。太監為難，要陳說笑以取樂，但只許說一個字，說笑了，便無罪放行。陳因脫口說了一個屁字，太監說，屁有甚麼好笑。陳說：「公公，我陳因這個屁，放由你，不放也由你。」太監笑了，也放了陳因這個屁。

張大千的香艷謎語

奴本是深閨弱質，生來白玉無瑕，遇那風流子弟，把奴家帶到黑暗處去玩耍，任他翻雲覆雨，上上下下，心滿意足，那時才把奴家放下。唉呀！那無情的冤家，臨行時，又將奴家一插。

——謎底：　毛筆

數學老師的電話號碼　　　Chistes de tutifruti

「你的電話號碼是⋯⋯？」甲師問。

「我的電話有六位數，請記下：第三位數是第一位數的三倍，第四和第六位數相同，第二位數是第五位數加一，六位數的總和等於二十三，相乘的結果等於二千一百六十。」

「二五六三四三。」乙師隨口回答。

「很好，記得嗎？」甲師不放心。

「容易，容易，前三位數等於十六的平方，後三位數等於七的立方。」

聰明的死刑犯　　The Gary McKee Hometown Radio Show

三個被判死刑的犯人，都誇耀自己聰明。行刑時，法官把甲犯送上電椅，連按三下電紐，死人電椅都沒有動靜，於是把他放了。

法官又把乙犯送上電椅，因為斷流，電椅還是不動，又把他放了。

法官再把丙犯送上電椅，按了一下電紐，電椅仍舊不動。法官還沒有動手再按電紐，丙犯已按耐不住：「怎麼搞的，你們沒有看到牆邊脫落的電線嗎？把它們接起來，電流不就來了！」

法官恍然大悟，也照辦了。

划船比賽　　　　　One to One

日航與美航划船團隊，舉行了一場比賽，結果日航超前一里而獲勝。美航立即聘請顧問公司，進行研究分析。時經三個月，報告出爐，問題出於日隊由一人指揮，八人划船；而美隊則有六人指揮，三人划船。

美航於是改組划船團隊，指派一位高級指揮，三位副指揮，四位顧問，一位划船手。

三個月以後，兩隊再賽，美隊又落敗，與日隊相去三里。美航耿耿於懷，開除了划船手，而他正是一位笨蛋老中。

SEMEN MISUSED　　　　The Washington Post

Peter Wallis and Kellie Smith fell in love. Later when Smith was pregnant, they split up. One year after their baby girl was born, Wallis sued Smith for becoming pregnant against his will, accusing her of "intentionally acquiring and misusing" his semen when they had sexual intercourse.

THE RYE BREAD WORKS

An old guy lost his potency sometimes ago. He

went to a Chinese herbalist who said that the gland of the monkey would help him improve his capability, but it was very expensive. The doctor told him not to worry about it.

"I heard that the rye bread works just as well." He said. So the guy rushed to a Jewish delicatessen and asked for twelve loaves of rye bread.

"Are you going to have a party?" The women behind the counter asked him. "It will become hard before you finish it."

"Why does everyone know about the bread but me?" The guy wondered.

BLUSH HOUR — Jakie Roberts

I did laundry for my mother and labelled her sheets with tapes. Once I was in a hurry, grabbed a tape for my mother's sheets, and stuck it on my shirt. Later, I stopped at a gas station, where I noticed the man behind the counter staring at me. As soon as I got back to my car, I looked down at my chest. There in block letters were the words:

SINGLE, BOTTOM FITTED.

THE WEIRD

-- Reported by Ann Landers

In Miami, a tiny Chihuahua and a large Rottweiler fell in love. The veterinarian performed a hysterectomy because he believed it would be a hazardous pregnancy.

In Guyana, police officers had to step in to curtail the activities of a monkey who had been breaking into homes, putting on lipstick, and condoms and upsetting people with his rude gestures and lewd dancing.

In Harmony, Texas, an agriculture teacher was fired after he allowed a student to castrate a pig with his teeth.

In Ottawa, a man learned not to stick his nose into other people's business after an angry passenger bit off a portion of his nose when he tried to stop a fight between the passenger and a taxi driver.

The wife of a Portuguese woman was charged with fraud after spending 20 years pretending to be a male general in the army -- uniform, chauffeur and all. "I never suspected anything," the hapless spouse told the court.

MY CHAUFFEUR CAN ANSWER

-- Kumiko Yoshida

A scientist went to a lecture. His chauffeur suggested to him, "Doc, I have heard your speech many times. I believe I can do it for you and you can take a break tonight."

The scientist agreed.

When they got to the conference room, the scientist put on his chauffeur's hat and sat in the back row. His chauffeur walked to the lectern and delivered the speech. At the end, he asked if there were questions.

"Yes," one professor in the front row raised his hand. "In your investigation, you mentioned Delphi method, can you elaborate it a little bit?"

The chauffeur was panic at the unexpected question, but he quickly recovered. "It's a simple question. My chauffeur can explain it to you."

IT'S GOD'S PLAN

— Original source lost

When troubles come and things go wrong,
  and days are cheerless and nights are long,
    you find it so easy to give in to despair
    by magnifying the burdens you bears.
You add to your worries by refusing to try
  to look for the rainbow in an overcast sky.
And the blessing God sent in a darkened
  disguise your troubled heart fail to
  recognize.
Not knowing God sent it not to distress you
  but to strengthen your faith and redeem
  you and bless you.
It's easy to grow downhearted
  when nothing goes your way.
It's easy to be discouraged
  when you have a troublesome day,
But trouble is only a challenge
  to spur you to achieve the best
  that God has to offer

if you have the faith to believe!
Life is a highway
on which the years go by.
Sometimes the road is level.
Sometimes the hills are high.
But as you travel onward
to a future that's unknown,
you can make each mile you travel
a heavenly stepping stone.
God is the master builder.
His plans are perfect and true.
And when He sends you sorrow,
it's part of His plan for you.
For all things work together
to complete the master plan.
And God up in His heaven
can see what's best for man.

索 引

INDEX

T-Z

國家圖書館出版品預行編目

東鱗西爪 ＝ The patches of light clouds /
　王之著. -- 一版. -- 臺北市：秀威資訊科
技, 2005[民 94]
　　面 ；　公分. -- (語言文學類；PG0045)
　含索引
　ISBN 978-986-7263-02-5(平裝)

855　　　　　　　　　　　94001774

語言文學類　PG0045

東鱗西爪

作　　者 / 王之
發 行 人 / 宋政坤
執行編輯 / 李坤城
圖文排版 / 張家禎
封面設計 / 羅季芬
數位轉譯 / 徐真玉　沈裕閔
圖書銷售 / 林怡君
法律顧問 / 毛國樑　律師
出版印製 / 秀威資訊科技股份有限公司
　　　　　台北市內湖區瑞光路 583 巷 25 號 1 樓
　　　　　電話：02-2657-9211　　　傳真：02-2657-9106
　　　　　E-mail：service@showwe.com.tw
經 銷 商 / 紅螞蟻圖書有限公司
　　　　　台北市內湖區舊宗路二段 121 巷 28、32 號 4 樓
　　　　　電話：02-2795-3656　　　傳真：02-2795-4100
　　　　　http://www.e-redant.com

2005 年 3 月 BOD 一版
定價：400 元

讀 者 回 函 卡

感謝您購買本書，為提升服務品質，煩請填寫以下問卷，收到您的寶貴意見後，我們會仔細收藏記錄並回贈紀念品，謝謝！

1.您購買的書名：＿＿＿＿＿＿＿＿＿＿＿＿＿＿＿＿＿＿＿＿

2.您從何得知本書的消息？

　　□網路書店　　□部落格　　□資料庫搜尋　　□書訊　　□電子報　　□書店

　　□平面媒體　　□ 朋友推薦　　□網站推薦　□其他＿＿＿＿＿＿＿

3.您對本書的評價：(請填代號　1.非常滿意 2.滿意 3.尚可 4.再改進)

　　封面設計＿＿　版面編排＿＿＿　內容＿＿＿　文/譯筆＿＿＿　價格＿＿＿

4.讀完書後您覺得：

　　□很有收獲　　□有收獲　　□收獲不多　　□沒收獲

5.您會推薦本書給朋友嗎？

　　□會　□不會，為什麼？＿＿＿＿＿＿＿＿＿＿＿＿＿＿＿＿＿＿＿＿＿＿

6.其他寶貴的意見：＿＿＿＿＿＿＿＿＿＿＿＿＿＿＿＿＿＿＿＿＿＿＿＿＿＿

＿＿＿＿＿＿＿＿＿＿＿＿＿＿＿＿＿＿＿＿＿＿＿＿＿＿＿＿＿＿＿＿＿＿＿

＿＿＿＿＿＿＿＿＿＿＿＿＿＿＿＿＿＿＿＿＿＿＿＿＿＿＿＿＿＿＿＿＿＿＿

＿＿＿＿＿＿＿＿＿＿＿＿＿＿＿＿＿＿＿＿＿＿＿＿＿＿＿＿＿＿＿＿＿＿＿

讀者基本資料

姓名：＿＿＿＿＿＿＿＿＿＿＿　年齡：＿＿＿＿　性別：□女　□男

聯絡電話：＿＿＿＿＿＿＿＿＿　E-mail：＿＿＿＿＿＿＿＿＿＿＿＿＿

地址：＿＿＿＿＿＿＿＿＿＿＿＿＿＿＿＿＿＿＿＿＿＿＿＿＿＿＿＿＿＿＿

學歷：□高中(含)以下　　　□高中　　　□專科學校　　　□大學

　　　□研究所(含)以上　□其他＿＿＿＿＿＿＿＿＿

職業：□製造業　□金融業　□資訊業　□軍警　□傳播業　□自由業

　　　□服務業　□公務員　□教職　　□學生　□其他＿＿＿＿＿＿